Once upon a time there lived the Marriage Makers—three fairy godmothers. Their job was to look after all the triplets in their domain, including the Knight triplets. One by one each fairy sprinkled her dust...

And baby Ryan got an overdose of humor and stubbornness! He just became *Too Stubborn To Marry.*

"Cathie's writing always glows with warmth and charm."
—Jayne Ann Krentz

"Cathie is a great storyteller."
—Lass Small

"Love and laughter is never more delightful than from the clever pen of Cathie Linz."
—Melinda Helfer

Dear Reader,

The comic antics continue with two very different but equally wonderful romantic comedies!

Longtime reader favorite Cathie Linz has joined the LOVE & LAUGHTER lineup with a very special trilogy called MARRIAGE MAKERS. Susan Elizabeth Phillips says, "Cathie Linz's fun and lively romances are guaranteed to win readers' hearts! A shining star of the romance genre." Jennifer Greene adds, "Every book has sparkle and wit; Cathie is truly a unique voice in the genre." Cathie is also the winner of the *Romantic Times* Storyteller of the Year Award, as well as being nominated for Career Achievement in Love and Laughter. Her trilogy about the Knight triplets includes lots of emotion, comedy and the antics of some well-intentioned but bumbling fairy godmothers.

Jule McBride spins a fabulous tale in *How the West Was Wed,* part of our Western mini marathon. A three-time Reviewer's Choice nominee for "Best American Romance," Jule McBride has also been nominated for two lifetime achievement awards in the category of "Love and Laughter." When Jule, a native of West Virginia, was little she kept her books inside her grandmother Helen's carved oak cabinet, to which only she had the key. Only later did Jule realize that the characters she loved weren't real and that someone called a "writer" conjured them. That's when she knew one day she'd be a writer. And Jule has created very memorable and hilarious characters in this story of a cross-dressing cowboy! (Really, he's the hero. It's fun— think Tom Hanks and Robin Williams.)

Enjoy the love and laughter,

Malle Vallik

Malle Vallik
Associate Senior Editor

Too Stubborn To Marry
Cathie Linz

Harlequin Books

TORONTO • NEW YORK • LONDON
AMSTERDAM • PARIS • SYDNEY • HAMBURG
STOCKHOLM • ATHENS • TOKYO • MILAN
MADRID • WARSAW • BUDAPEST • AUCKLAND

ISBN 0-373-44045-6

TOO STUBBORN TO MARRY

Copyright © 1998 by Cathie L. Baumgardner

Dear Reader,

I write books to make readers smile, to make them laugh. That's why I'm honored to be a double nominee for a *Romantic Times* Love and Laughter award and delighted by the invitation to do this special trilogy for Harlequin's LOVE & LAUGHTER.

I figure we could all use a little more laughter in our lives, right? I don't know of anyone who says, "No, thanks, I've got all the laughter I can handle right now, thank you, anyway."

Too much stress, yes. Too much laughter? Naw. Although I do remember this one time when I was ten and I laughed so hard my best friend and I spewed chocolate milk all over the dainty pink-and-white-striped wallpaper we were supposed to be helping my mom put up. But that's another story...and I plan on using it in the final book in this trilogy.

For now, sit back, kick off your shoes, keep those chocolate chip cookies handy (but be careful with the chocolate milk!) and be prepared to meet a man who is too stubborn to wed and the woman who captures his heart. I hope you fall for Deputy U.S. Marshal Ryan Knight the way both Courtney and I did! We both seem to have a weakness for a man *out* of uniform (grin).

Happy reading,

Cathie Linz

For my editor,
Malle Vallik,
who hears the
creative voices and
understands the
magic of the process.

Prologue

"OKAY, ARE YOU ready for our next assignment?" Betty Goodie demanded of her two sisters, shoving the snowy white bangs of her Prince Valiant haircut off her forehead.

"As ready as I'll ever be." Muriel's voice quavered nervously.

"We're fairy godmothers," Hattie stated firmly, shifting the chirping canary perched on the crown of her lemon yellow hat. In the process, she nearly poked out her eye with her color-coordinated magic wand. If there was one thing Hattie prided herself on, it was her ability to accessorize. "It's our job to be ready...for anything."

The three sisters were gathered at their prearranged meeting place. Ryan Knight's bedroom in the middle of the night. Moonlight was their only illumination. Betty was perched atop a blue lamp shade while Muriel chose to do her pacing on the pine headboard of Ryan's bed.

Hattie, meanwhile, was doing her primping from above. She'd taken over one blade of the stationary ceiling fan. She loved being higher than anyone else.

"You claim we should be ready for anything, but we weren't ready for what happened at the Knight triplets' christening thirty-three years ago,'' Muriel, the practical one in the family, recalled.

"Don't remind me." Hattie shuddered, removing her hat to run nervous fingers through her silvery curls before jamming her overstated headgear back on her head. The canary chirped in protest. "First, Betty messed up by spilling too much common sense and sex appeal fairy dust on baby Jason Knight, then you also blundered and spilled too much stubborness and humor fairy dust on baby Ryan Knight."

"And then *you* really screwed up and splattered an overdose of intelligence and attitude fairy dust on baby Anastasia," Muriel interjected.

"I did not screw up!" Hattie declared indignantly. "I merely made a *slight* miscalculation. I was still a novice at flying in those days. I'm much better at it now." To prove her point, she batted her petite gossamer wings and left her perch on the fan to perform a perfect midair somersault before daintily flitting to the open doorway and back again.

"Show-off!" Muriel scoffed.

"Fussbudget!" Hattie retorted.

"No fighting, girls." The brusque order came from Betty, who was the oldest of the Goodie triplets by ninety seconds and therefore considered herself to be the leader of their group. "Now that we've accomplished our goals with his brother, it's time to turn our attention to Ryan."

Muriel paused from her pacing long enough to gaze down at their charge, who was sound asleep. Peering through the darkness, she made her magic wand glow with magical fairy light in an attempt to get a better view. "He doesn't look like he'd cause any trouble."

"Hah!" Hattie was clearly skeptical. "Looks are deceptive. Remember, thanks to you, Ryan got too much from the stubbornness and humor end of the characteristic scales."

Muriel bragged, "His practical jokes are famous."

"More like *infamous,*" Betty noted.

"Are you sure he didn't get too much sloppiness, not stubbornness?" Hattie looked around the messy bedroom with censure. Clothing was haphazardly tossed over a chair while the leg of a pair of jeans trailed onto the floor. There was no empty space on top of the cluttered dresser, which is why Betty had been forced to perch atop the lamp shade. The pine floor was littered with a damp bath towel and several magazines, among other things.

"He's a guy," Muriel defended him.

"His brother, Jason, is a guy," Hattie argued, "and he is extremely neat."

Betty rejoined the conversation. "The neater they are, the harder they fall," she firmly maintained. "Our work with Jason is done. We united him with his soul mate. Now we have to do the same with Ryan."

"I still say that a grape jelly jar is no place for you to keep something as magical as fairy dust." Hattie's soft musical voice was laced with disapproval.

Betty was unrepentant. "I don't use a grape jelly jar anymore." She deliberately paused a beat before adding, "I've switched to strawberry. And I only bring that out at christenings, so don't get your wings in a knot.''

Hattie stamped her foot, her high heels clicking on the polished fan blade. "I keep telling you and Muriel that you two don't show enough respect for the importance of what we do. Fairy godmothers are an institution. We don't fall into the paranormal realm like witches. We're...*mythical.*'' Hattie said the word with great reverence.

"I'll tell you what's mythical,'' Muriel retorted. "The concept of time off. I say we need a union to get better working hours and benefits. Look at what happened to our predecessors.''

Hattie shot her an exasperated look. "Our predecessors retired after 250 years and are doing just fine.'' Frowning, she added the reprimand, "You've never taken our jobs seriously.''

"Hey, I wasn't the one who thought being a fairy godmother would be a lark.''

"Yes, you were,'' Hattie maintained. "You and Betty both.''

"That was only to cheer you up,'' Muriel said, "after it was too late to change things. The truth is, we wouldn't be in this mess if you hadn't gotten in the wrong line in heaven. If you'd put on your glasses instead of being so vain, you would have read the sign and seen that we were at the wrong location.''

"You were the one who liked that line because it was shorter than the others.''

"We learned why.'' Muriel shoved an impatient hand through the spiky tufts of her short white hair, making her cowlick stick up even worse than usual and giving her the appearance of a woodpecker. "This fairy godmothering business is hard work."

"I would have preferred being a guardian angel," Hattie confessed. "Their wings are so much more elegant looking. And they're taller."

"Their wings are taller?" Muriel asked.

"No." Hattie frowned, before remembering that it caused wrinkles. She had enough of those. "The angels are taller than we are."

"Crickets are taller than we are," Muriel said.

Betty clapped her hands to regain their attention. "Enough with the ancient history already. We don't have time for this."

A snore from below startled them all, reminding them of their purpose. Three pairs of blue fairy godmothers' eyes honed in on Ryan.

He slept on his right side. His tousled head lay on the pillow in such a way as to give them a good look at his profile; his high forehead, heavy brows, thick lashes on lean cheekbones, the noble nose and curved expressive lips. The rumpled comforter covered a body that was slim but as strong as steel. One muscular forearm, dappled with dark hair, was flung across the bottom sheet as if he were reaching for something—or someone—in his sleep.

"Well, he's not quite as good-looking as his brother." This proclamation came from Hattie, who put a great deal of stock in appearances.

"Stop picking on him." Muriel flew down to the base of the bed to direct her magic wand toward Ryan's bare foot. On command, the denim comforter covering the rest of him shifted to cover his foot as well. "I like him."

"I like him, too," Hattie said. "It's obvious from the lines on his face that he laughs a lot."

"Thanks to me." Muriel proudly threw back her shoulders, thereby displaying her ample bosom clothed in a white shirt and photographer's vest.

"He's also got a stubborn streak a mile long thanks to you," Betty reminded her. "Remember how he did a lot of the work on this house himself when he first moved in here, stubbornly refusing to call in a plumber to repair that leaky gas pipe."

"And almost blew himself up in the process," Hattie added.

"I think he's learned his lesson since then," Muriel loyally declared.

Betty didn't look so sure. "Regarding home repairs, maybe. Not his love life."

"He doesn't have much of a love life," Muriel noted, "not with his job as a U.S. Marshal."

"Deputy U.S. Marshal," Hattie corrected.

"Picky, picky." Muriel stuck out her tongue.

"Enough." Betty clapped her hands imperiously. "No more bickering. Let's get down to work here."

1

"WHY DON'T YOU just shoot me now instead?" Deputy U.S. Marshal Ryan Knight said to his boss, Wes Freeze.

"Shoot you?" Taking his time, Wes leaned farther back in his office chair and fixed Ryan with his trademark steely-eyed scrutiny. "Nah," he murmured slowly, his voice laced with enjoyment. "I'd rather just torture you slowly and watch you squirm."

"This will definitely make me squirm," Ryan assured him, leaning forward in his chair to make his point. At thirty-three, he'd run into his share of trouble and knew his strengths...and his weaknesses. "Trust me, I'm not the right man for this job."

"Trust *you?* As in the time you said to trust you, no one was going to do anything wild on my birthday this year?"

"Hey," Ryan protested, "I didn't think hiring that bag lady comedienne to do a roast about your life was all that wild."

"Compared to what? The year before when you convinced me that I'd won a million dollars in a magazine contest?"

Ryan couldn't stop the brief smile. "You've got to admit that the guys did a great job making those documents looks official. Even the van was authentic, down to the Prize Patrol lettering on the side."

"I don't have to admit anything, except that you made me look like a damn fool," Wes growled.

Ryan shifted uncomfortably. "That was never my intention, sir."

Wes's office in the Portland district office felt as if it were getting smaller by the second. Sitting there facing his disapproving boss, Ryan suddenly recalled facing an equally unappreciative principal back at Chicago's Lincoln High School. Even then Ryan's practical jokes were legendary and were no more appreciated by the principal than they were by Wes now. But then Ryan considered neither man was exactly known for his well-developed sense of humor.

"Let's get back to the matter at hand, shall we?" Wes tapped his index finger on the open manila folder on his desk. "After only two hours in protective custody Anton Leva took off."

Ryan could feel his facial muscles tightening. "I accept full responsibility for his escape happening on my watch."

"Good. I'm glad to hear that. Although how he managed to squeeze out that dinky bathroom window, I have no idea," Wes drawled with a shake of his head. "Had to be like threading rope through the eye of a needle." Wes fixed that steely-eyed gaze on Ryan once again, and Ryan resisted the urge to squirm. "We need him back to testify in the Zopo brothers counterfeiting case. The U.S. Attorney's office is not amused that you lost their chief material witness. And frankly I'm not laughing, either. Something like this doesn't make our office look good. I want it cleared up. I want Leva apprehended.'' Wes's lips twitched in what could have been a smile. ''Given his close ties with his niece, Courtney Delaney, it's only a matter of time before he contacts her. After all, she is his only living relative and she's right here in the Portland area.''

Damn his luck, Ryan thought. He'd only been given the Anton Leva assignment after another deputy had called in sick. And damn his luck that Courtney was involved. The last time he'd seen her had been back in Chicago.

''So I want you to stick close to this woman,'' Wes continued. ''The Zopo brothers could use Ms. Delaney to get to Leva.''

''I understand that, sir. And, believe me, no one wants Anton back or Courtney kept safe more than I do.'' The thought of her being in danger made Ryan's blood run cold. The problem was that the idea of seeing her again made his body hot and bothered. He and Courtney had been lovers. Their breakup three years ago had been as passionate and stormy as their relationship. ''Given my previous history with her, it might be better to have a female deputy interview Courtney. She'd probably be more willing to talk to her, given that bonding thing that goes on between women.''

''That previous history is precisely why I chose you. That and a chance for you to redeem yourself. Besides, I don't have a female deputy available right now for...*bonding*.'' Wes's mocking voice clearly displayed his irritation. "You're the best deputy in the Northwest. You and I both know it."

"Courtney isn't going to like me showing up."

"She doesn't have to like it. Neither do you. What with LeSoto on family leave and Matsumo out sick, we're short staffed. So *you're* to provide protection to Ms. Delaney, if needed, while using her to locate Leva. You caused this mess by letting Anton Leva slip away, you clean it up." Wes's authoritative tone left no room for argument. "Have I made myself clear?"

"Yes, sir."

"Good. Oh, and Ryan, just so you know. I plan on being out of town on my next birthday."

Ryan sighed. "Understood, sir."

RYAN LINGERED OVER a second cup of coffee in the only diner which happened to be located across from the only bank in Fell, Oregon. The small town was about an hour east of Portland. Courtney lived here, and had for the past year. So close and yet so far away.

Whenever he'd thought of Courtney, and he had thought of her plenty, he had pictured her where he'd left her, back in the urban energy of Chicago.

Anton hadn't said a word about his niece having moved to the Northwest. In fact, Anton hadn't said much at all. Ryan hadn't even been sure the other man had recognized him. But Ryan had recognized Anton, which is why he'd let down his guard.

It wouldn't happen again. Anton might look like a shaggy Jimmy Stewart, but he was no Mr. Nice Guy.

He was contradictory and complicated. Just like his niece.

A gorgeous blonde with brown eyes, Courtney was emotional, energetic, and passionate. When Ryan had met her, she'd been dealing cards on a riverboat casino outside of Chicago. He'd been twenty-seven and she'd been twenty-five.

The attraction had been instant and intense. She'd accepted his invitation to go out with him, but hadn't let him kiss her until their third date. Three months later, she'd moved in with him.

Life with Courtney had never been dull. She'd loved him like he was the only man in the world for her and then she'd left him because he'd decided to join the U.S. Marshals Service.

Women. If he lived to be a hundred, he'd never understand them. He'd wanted to make her proud of him, therefore, he hadn't told Courtney about his plans, until he'd learned he'd passed the tough entrance exam and been accepted into the service. Instead of being proud of him, she'd had a fit and walked out.

He hadn't gone after her. A man had his pride. *She'd* left *him.* All he'd done was pursue his dream of being a marshal, a dream he'd had long before he'd met Courtney. Besides, only a fool loved a woman who hated his job. Still, he'd never forgotten her....

"You need a refill?" the friendly waitress asked him with a flirtatious smile.

"No, thanks." It was time to get off his duff and take his medicine like a man.

Problem was, he'd never met a woman who made

him feel like more of a man than Courtney. But the man wasn't going to see her, the Deputy U.S. Marshal was.

IT HAD BEEN a slow afternoon, even for a Saturday at the Fell Federal Bank. Working as a bank teller wasn't the most exciting job Courtney had ever had, and she'd had plenty. But then she wasn't looking for excitement any longer.

Actually she was now an assistant savings officer, having just been promoted the week before. The difference in pay wasn't huge, but anything was appreciated at this point. Courtney wasn't exactly living the life-style of the rich and famous here, more like the nearly broke and inconsequential. After she paid her rent and utilities, there wasn't much of her paycheck left over.

And then there was Francis Grimshaw breathing down her neck as she monitored Courtney's work in the savings department. Petite and scarecrow thin, Francis was a perfectionist. She wore her gray hair cropped short and never had a strand out of place. As assistant manager, Francis made it her business to supervise everything, which didn't make her the most popular person around. Always looking like she'd just sucked on a lemon didn't help either.

Courtney suspected that Francis was actually a very lonely woman, so she'd gone out of her way to be nice to her. Not that the other woman gave any sign of noticing. If anything, it was almost as if Francis became even more suspicious of Courtney's kindness.

In an attempt to keep busy, Courtney finished

sharpening the last of her five pencils and set them on her desk in a neat row as she'd been instructed to do in Francis's regimented by-the-book training. One of the pencils broke free and made a run for freedom, rolling off her desk.

"I'd made a break for it, too, if I were you," Courtney murmured as she leaned under her desk to retrieve it.

Of course the blasted thing had rolled completely under the desk, requiring her to get down on her hands and knees. She would have left the fugitive where it lay, but Francis counted the pencils at the end of the day and if too many were missing the disgrace was noted on the employee's record. Courtney had already lost a dozen pencils in her first week; she suspected the sticky-fingered customers.

Not that Francis had bought that story. She was convinced Courtney was hoarding pencils. No doubt Francis suspected her of selling them to make a profit.

From her cubbyhole beneath the desk, Courtney she saw a pair of male shoes come into view. They weren't the shiny leather shoes of a businessman, they were big-ticket running shoes worn for comfort. And they were standing directly in front of her desk. Which meant *someone* was standing in front of her desk, while she was scrounging around under it.

Curses!

Hurriedly backing up, she narrowly avoided banging her head on the bottom of the drawer as she sat up. The blood rushed to her head at straightening so quickly, but she still managed to summon a smile. "Can I help...*you?!*"

Ryan Knight, the man she'd given her heart to only to have him stomp all over it, showed no such surprise at seeing her.

She blinked, thinking perhaps she'd conjured him up because of light-headedness. No such luck. He was still standing in front of her when she opened her eyes a moment later.

He'd been everything to her, and meant everything. He'd starred in all her dreams, answered all her hopes.

The last time she'd seen him had been in the pouring rain in Chicago. She'd tried to wipe the words from her memory but they still remained, three years later. "This isn't about you, it's about *me,*" he'd shouted. "About *my* future."

Even now, she had the strongest urge to leap across the sedate oak desk, grab him by the collar of his flannel shirt and demand to know why he'd had to break her heart. And why did he have to look better now than he had three years ago? What was he doing in Oregon? Why couldn't he have stayed in Chicago? Why couldn't he have gained fifty pounds and gotten a beer belly? Was there no poetic justice?

Apparently not. His low-pitched voice was as seductive as ever. "Nice to see you again, Courtney. You're looking—" he quirked an eyebrow at her "—different."

She glared at him, still knowing him well enough to know that his words were no compliment. She was well aware that she looked rather washed-out in the plain beige suit she wore with a prim white blouse. Her long blond hair was twisted into a tight knot on top of her head. She knew she wouldn't win any fashion awards, but this was how she was expected to dress for her job now. Conservative attire was a requirement at the Fell Federal Bank.

Apparently the same right-wing dress code didn't apply to U.S. Marshals. He was casually dressed, looking ruggedly handsome in jeans and an open flannel shirt with a T-shirt underneath, standard attire for men in the Northwest. It didn't look at all standard on Ryan. Her anger rose. Why had he shown up now, after all this time? Unless...

Could it be? Was it possible that he'd tracked her down to declare his love for her, to say how sorry he was to have let her go, that he wanted her back? For months after their breakup, she'd dreamed of that. Had it really come to happen? She couldn't speak.

"Is there a problem here?" Francis inquired as she hovered over them like a hyperactive hen.

"No problem," Ryan answered on Courtney's behalf. "You're lucky to have a diligent employee like Ms. Delaney working here at your bank."

Francis didn't know what to make of that, so she made do with a humph noise, meant to be innocuous without offering agreement. Slowly she returned to her own desk—out of eavesdropping range.

Courtney gave Ryan her perkiest employee-of-the-month smile as he plunked himself down onto the chair across from her. "What are you doing here?"

If he was going to declare his love, now was the time. It could happen, it could...

"I'm here on business."

The wild fantasy came crashing down. Nothing had

changed. Ryan's work still came first. Which was fine by her. She'd moved on, figuratively and literally.

"I don't have any business with the U.S. Marshals Service. Is this one of your warped practical jokes?"

"Does it look like I'm laughing?"

No, not at the moment, although it looked like he'd gotten more laugh lines at the corners of his eyes since she'd seen him last. Ryan had never been as classically handsome as his brother, Jason. But he had a rugged look that grabbed your attention and kept it. His face was angular, his brows wide. His brown hair had never obeyed the commands of a comb and it still showed an inclination to rebel.

As for his mouth... She used to tease him that it was crooked, listing just a tad to the left. He'd respond by kissing her until she begged for mercy.

Curses, he was here only five minutes and already she was thinking of orgasms? This wouldn't do at all!

"How did you find me?" She managed to get the question out without it sounding too breathless.

"It wasn't difficult. I'm here on official business." Taking out his wallet, he showed her his badge. "When was the last time you saw your uncle?"

"Uncle Anton?"

"That's right, your uncle Anton." Ryan's expression reflected his exasperation. "The *only* uncle you have."

"Why do you want to know?" Experience had taught her to be cautious giving out any information about her unconventional relative.

"I'm asking the questions."

"And I'm not answering them." Her uncle had

raised her after her parents had died in a car crash when she was ten. Since then, she and he had lived in twenty different states. Before immigrating to the U.S., Anton had been an actor in Prague and he'd retained his flair for the dramatic, passing it on to Courtney—along with a love for music by Dvořák, Smetana and, in tribute to his new country, the Everly Brothers.

Uncle Anton had done everything from selling vacuum cleaners to managing a print shop. In between he'd been involved in a few slightly shady dealings. While he may have bent the law a little, he'd certainly never actually broken it.

"What do you want with my uncle?" Courtney wasn't sure she wanted to know the answer.

"He's a material witness in a federal trial."

"A witness to what?"

"He hasn't told you about this?" Ryan arched an eyebrow at her. "I find that hard to believe, given how close the two of you are."

"You and I were close once, that didn't mean we knew everything about each other," she said icily. "In fact, you turned out to be very different from the man I thought you were."

"I'm not here to talk about me. I'm here because of your uncle. And because you might be in danger."

"From Uncle Anton? Never!"

"Not from him, no. From the people he's testifying against. The Zopo brothers."

She couldn't help it. The name made her smile. "You're kidding, right?"

"Nope." A flash of humor gleamed in Ryan's hazel eyes. "Brutus and Caesar Zopo. Seems their mom was a big fan of ancient Roman history."

Ancient history was what she and Ryan were. Now her thoughts had to remain focused on her uncle and his safety. "What did you get my uncle into?"

Ryan looked at her in surprise. *"Me?"*

"United States Marshals are supposed to provide personal protection to important witnesses."

"Most people don't know that."

"I checked into it when you snuck out and took that entrance exam behind my back. I wanted to know what would make you go from something as secure as corporate security to a bounty-hunting job like the U.S. Marshals Service."

"I did not sneak out behind your back and we're not bounty hunters."

She stuck to her guns. "You most certainly did. You didn't tell me anything about what you were up to. But that's not relevant. Right now my only concern is my uncle."

"Same here. We want to track him down as quickly as possible."

"My uncle isn't some kind of wildlife that you *track down.* How did you lose him? And what did you threaten him with to make him agree to be a material witness in the first place?" Courtney bristled with indignation. "My uncle avoids the authorities like the plague. A material witness to what?"

"To counterfeiting."

His answer filled her with astonishment. "My uncle is not a counterfeiter."

"I never said he was." In contrast to hers, Ryan's

voice was calm. "But he worked for people who are suspected of being in charge of a large counterfeiting ring."

Courtney restrained the urge to hoot in derision. "My uncle managed a print shop. What happened, did someone photocopy a ten-dollar bill?"

"No," he replied, "the Zopos forged a million dollars worth of cashiers' checks. And they own the print shop your uncle worked in."

Courtney didn't know what to say. It was true that her uncle wasn't always the best judge of character. But then who was she to throw stones? She'd thought Ryan was a man of honor, a man who was as true as the day was long.

"I haven't heard from my uncle in a week," she said with obvious reluctance and more than a hint of anxiety. "When did you lose him?"

"He's only been missing for six hours." His voice was curt.

"Then go out and find him and protect him." *And stay away from me,* she silently continued. *Far away. Japan would be nice.*

"I do plan on finding him. By staying close to you."

Ryan's words struck fear in her heart. "I've told you, I don't know where he is."

"I heard you the first time. And you may be telling the truth."

"*May* be?" Her voice rose, gaining Francis's attention.

Ryan waved the older woman away with a smile and a few loudly voiced assurances. "We're doing fine here. Talking about the wisdom of investing my money in a bank, that it *may* be safer than stocks. Ms. Delaney is assuring me it is safer.''

''She's right.'' Francis looked as if she wanted to say more, but Ryan turned his back on her as he leaned across the desk to speak to Courtney once again.

''Look, I don't like this any more than you do,'' he informed her. ''But the bottom line is that I'm not leaving your side until your uncle is back in my custody.''

Their gazes were locked in silent combat a moment or two before Courtney vocalized her feelings. ''Over my dead body!''

''STILL THINK THAT dealing with Ryan and Courtney is going to be easy?'' Betty Goodie mocked her sister Muriel as they both perched on a black file cabinet in the corner of the bank's savings department surveying the heated exchange between Courtney and Ryan.

''Nothing seems to be easy about being a fairy godmother,'' Muriel noted glumly, her blue eyes flashing in her weathered face. ''Especially being a fairy godmother for triplets.''

''Don't blame it on them being triplets.'' Betty impatiently shoved her white bangs out of her eyes by using the tip of her magic wand. ''We were triplets and we were never this much trouble to anyone.''

''We still *are* triplets,'' the ever practical Muriel corrected. ''And goodness knows what trouble we caused in our day.''

''I can't believe how they've decorated this place,''

Hattie declared, entering the conversation for the first time. Holding up a gilded hand mirror, she quickly checked her appearance, as if afraid her dreary surroundings might wear off on her. She patted her silvery curls and rearranged the wide brim on her fuchsia-colored hat. Her nails and lipstick were a matching shade. Ditto for her frothy frock. "It looks more like a funeral parlor in here than a bank."

"Look at the guy running this place and you'll see why," Betty retorted. "Fred Finley is hardly the stylish type."

Hattie frowned. "Then why is Courtney dating him?"

"Because she wants security in her life," Betty explained. As the oldest she hated having to explain anything, preferring to give commands and be obeyed. "She's sworn off passion since she broke up with Ryan."

"I can't believe I'm supposed to bring these two back together after they split up. That's a tough gig, even for a fairy godmother. Doesn't seem fair to me," Muriel grumbled, reaching into one of the many pockets of her khaki photographer's vest for her bag of granola, her favorite munchie. "That's harder than having him meet someone new."

Hattie fixed her with a reprimanding look. "His soul mate is Courtney, not someone new."

"Then why didn't they stay together three years ago?" Muriel asked.

Betty answered. "Their time hadn't come." She tapped an oversize EZ-Read watch on her arm. "Now it has. So let's get moving."

"We already set things into motion by getting Anton to take off the way he did. I certainly hope we didn't put him in real danger," Hattie worried. "He was rather dreamy-looking, don't you think?"

"I think that we're going to have our hands full with this case," Betty replied.

"So what else is new?" Muriel muttered as she studied their two charges, standing practically nose to nose. "I should have gone into banking instead of fairy godmothering. The hours are definitely better."

2

"DON'T YOU THINK you're overreacting just a bit?"

Ryan's words made Courtney see red as she flashed back to the last time he'd said them to her—in the rain in Chicago. "You seem to have that effect on me."

Something dark and hungry flickered in his hazel eyes as he murmured, "I seem to recall having a better effect on you."

"That was a different woman."

"Apparently." He leaned back to give her the once-over. "The Courtney I knew wouldn't have been caught dead wearing a suit like that."

"The Courtney you knew doesn't exist anymore," she snapped. "Deal with it."

"Just like you'll have to deal with the fact that we're stuck with each other until I find your uncle."

Courtney didn't like the sound of that at all. "Define stuck with each other."

"I plan on being your shadow. Where you go, I go."

She refused to let his proclamation fill her with panic. The trick to dealing with Ryan was to stay cool, calm and collected. Hard to do when he drove her nuts, but she was determined to give it a try.

"You can't sit here in the bank day after day. I've already said that I don't know where my uncle is. I'll tell you what. Leave me your business card, and if he checks in with me I'll give you a call." If she thought it was in her uncle's best interest, which was a *big* if.

"Right," he scoffed. "And if I believe that, you've got some oceanfront property in Kansas you'd like to sell me real cheap. Forget it."

Her brown eyes flashed with anger, all thoughts of being cool or calm disappearing. "Are you saying you don't trust me?"

"I'm saying that you have a misguided sense of loyalty to your uncle and that may be clouding your judgment. Not that your judgment was ever the clearest."

"That was the old Courtney," she said caustically. "The one who misjudged you. The new Courtney has twenty-twenty judgment vision."

"If you say so." He clearly wasn't buying her claim. "The bottom line is that I have a job to do and I aim on doing it."

"I've got a job to do, too. And I can't do it with you getting in my way."

"Fine. Then I'll just sit over there—" he indicated a chair on the other side of the lobby "—until closing time. It's only a few minutes away. You close early on Saturdays, right?"

Courtney felt frustration eating away at her control. How dare Ryan order her around? "That might take care of today, but what about Monday? I'm telling you, you can't spy on me at work. There's no way I could explain your continued presence."

"Tell your boss I'm besotted with you and can't let you out of my sight."

Courtney snorted.

"You don't think she'd believe it?" Ryan demanded with feigned indignation. "I can look besotted if I need to. Here, watch." He opened his hazel eyes wide, as if to give her a better view of the smoldering passion in them. All he accomplished was making her more aware of the thickness of his eyelashes. The downward slope of his lids gave him bedroom eyes, while the crinkles in the corners indicated that this was a man who liked laughter.

Courtney refused to allow herself to be drawn in. "You look like a cross between a myopic Mr. Magoo and Pepe Le Pew."

"You're still a fan of classic cartoons?"

She nodded, adding, "Laughter is good for the soul. You aren't."

Ryan smacked his hand to his chest. "You wound me."

He'd wounded her plenty. And now he had the nerve to try to charm her when the truth was that he'd only looked her up because of his job. That damn job. It had been the reason they'd broken up.

No, that wasn't true. It had been the excuse, the reason was Ryan's insistence on doing his own thing and not involving her in his decisions. When he'd told her that his future had nothing to do with her, he'd made it clear that she had no real importance to him, that she was a warm body in his bed but not a partner in his life.

She'd wanted more. Damn it, she deserved more.

For the first few months after she'd walked out, she'd secretly hoped Ryan would see the light, that he'd be miserable without her and realize his mistake.

Looking at him now, she saw no signs of misery or heartbreak. Instead she saw six feet of muscular dynamite just waiting to be detonated. Well, she was no longer the kind of woman interested in playing with fire, let alone explosives. She'd learned her lesson well.

These days she wanted security not passion. Slow and steady wins the race. Which is why she'd worked hard to change her image, to damper her more dramatically outrageous side and restrain it in a buttoned-down beige suit. Here in Fell she was known as a quiet, well-behaved young woman, and that was exactly the way she wanted it.

Her card-dealing days were behind her. Her unconventional nomadic life-style was a thing of the past. She was ready to settle down. She wanted a family. She wanted roots.

Try as her uncle had, he hadn't been able to replace her parents. She could still remember the security she'd felt in her father's arms, the certainty she'd always had of her mother's love. And while she loved her uncle and he loved her, security and certainty didn't go with his personality.

He'd done his best. He'd always made her feel that she was important to him and that life was filled with endless possibilities, usually right around the next corner or over the stateline. They'd moved a lot. From New Jersey to Pennsylvania to Ohio to Michigan to Illinois and so on.

She'd moved enough. Back in Chicago she'd believed in possibilities, allowed passion to rule her life. The results had been a broken heart. Now it was time to grow up, time to settle down. She didn't want Ryan interfering with her plans and ruining the new life she'd made for herself.

"Can't you wait for me outside and then we can discuss this situation in private?" she demanded, aware of the suspicious looks Francis was darting her way.

"And have you slip out the back door?" Ryan mocked. "No way. I told you, I'm just doing my job."

"And getting a great deal of pleasure out of aggravating me. Look, I've got a new life here. I don't need you hanging around messing things up for me."

"Keep your voice down," he warned her, "or you'll have that dragon lady breathing down our necks again. If it will make you feel any better, I'll speak to the bank manager and explain my presence."

"No!" She grabbed Ryan's hand to stop him. How long had it been since she'd touched him? Too long, yet not long enough to have gotten over the rush of exhilaration. It was discouraging to think that after three years she was still susceptible to his touch.

And it wasn't even as if he'd been the first one to initiate the contact. No, she'd been the blockhead who'd done that. Who was still doing that, belatedly realizing she still had a hold on his hand. She released her grip so suddenly his hand dropped to her desktop with a thump. "I don't want Fred knowing about you.

I don't want him thinking I've done something to warrant the attention of the U.S. Marshals Service."

Ryan gave her a curious look. "Why would he think that?"

Before she could answer, a skinny blond-haired man wearing a finely cut suit, horn-rimmed glasses, and a supercilious manner joined them. Ryan disliked him on sight, probably because of the proprietary hand he placed on Courtney's shoulder and the way he leaned over her as if claiming his ownership.

Instead of shrugging the little pip-squeak off, Courtney actually gave him a glowing smile while gazing up at him as if he were God's gift to women.

"Everything under control here?"

The man's voice matched the rest of his appearance—condescending and nerdy at the same time.

"Yes, Fred," Courtney replied. "Everything is just fine."

"Ms. Grimshaw indicated you might be having trouble."

Ryan was certainly trouble, Courtney silently allowed, but she'd manage somehow. She didn't like the way he was glaring at Fred, though. That didn't bode well.

"It's my fault," Ryan stated.

You bet it is. Her thoughts quickly turned anxious as she wondered what Ryan would say next. Would he flash his badge in front of Fred?

"I haven't seen Courtney in so long," Ryan continued.

"And you are...?" Fred interrupted him to inquire.

"Ryan Knight."

"I'm Fred Finley." He held out his hand to Ryan. "I'm the bank manager. You and Courtney are acquainted then?"

"More than merely acquainted, we're very close."

Time for some immediate damage control, Courtney decided. "Of course we're close," she quickly interrupted. "He's my...brother."

"Brother?" Fred's sandy eyebrows rose. "You never told me you had a brother. His surname isn't the same as yours."

"He's my half brother."

"Which half?" was Ryan's muttered aside, which thankfully only Courtney heard.

"He's just passing through town," she added.

"And staying with my sister for a while."

Ryan's announcement made Fred frown. "Her apartment isn't very big, you know."

This time it was Ryan's turn to frown. "How do you know?"

"Fred knows everything." Courtney gave him a brilliant smile.

Ryan didn't like what he was seeing here. The guy with the pencil neck had a relationship with Courtney. What could she possibly see in Fred Finley? He was so staid he made tapioca look exotic. And his handshake had been limp and clammy.

The old Courtney Delaney would have stayed a mile away from a guy like Fred. Or she would have given him a Looney Tunes tie to spice up his image. She would never have gazed up at him as if he were the be-all and end-all of her life.

Had she really changed that much?

What did he expect? He'd known she wouldn't be pleased to see him after all this time. But he hadn't expected her to be so different from the fun-loving, passionate woman he'd left in Chicago. He could have sworn she didn't have a conservative bone in her body, but now he didn't know what to think. Except that he was upset to see the changes in her.

The geeky banker was speaking to him. "Well, it was nice meeting you, Ryan."

"Same here, Frank."

Courtney glared at him, showing a flash of her old fire. "It's *Fred*, not Frank."

Ryan shrugged. "Whatever."

After Fred had returned to his office, Ryan said, "Half brother? That was the best you could do? Why not tell him the truth?"

"That you're a pain in the butt?"

"That I was your first lover." Ryan took pleasure in the possessive sound of the word first.

"But not my last." It was a lie but Courtney wasn't about to give him the satisfaction of knowing that.

Gritting his teeth, Ryan's voice was brisk and all business. "I'll follow you home in my car. Don't try anything cute like trying to lose me. I know where you live."

"It's in the file you no doubt have on me. I wouldn't be surprised if you already knew the color of my bedsheets." Bad choice of words, she belatedly decided.

"Not yet."

"Not ever."

"If you say so."

"I do."

It had been so strange seeing Fred and Ryan standing side by side—her past and her future. Two men couldn't be more different. Ryan was rugged and powerful. His face looked lived-in. Fred, with his blond hair, pampered skin and meticulous manner, looked like a very pale and very distant imitation.

No, she corrected herself. Not even an imitation. Another type entirely. Lacking the raw masculinity of Ryan. Lacking the flashes of humor, the lopsided grin. Her response to Ryan overwhelmed her, sweeping through her bloodstream like a drug.

"You ready to leave?" Ryan demanded, tapping an impatient finger on the face of his watch. "The bank closed ten minutes ago."

"You're crazy if you think I'm going to let you stay in my apartment." If she was this susceptible to him in a public place like the bank, she could only imagine what it would it be like in the close confines of her tiny apartment.

Ryan shrugged. "It's my job."

"So you've said," she muttered, gathering her purse from the bottom drawer of her desk. "Why should I believe you?"

"You shouldn't." Ryan took her elbow as soon as she came around the desk and guided her toward the exit. "Feel free to call my boss to verify it if you'd like."

"I'll do that." She yanked her arm away from his hold. "As soon as I get home and have some privacy."

"That's right. There'll be just you and me."

As Ryan followed her home from work, he was glad to discover one thing that hadn't changed about Courtney—her car. She'd bought it used when he'd met her in Chicago, and it had had sixty-thousand-some miles on it then. He was willing to bet that the little red compact had to have doubled its mileage since then.

It was comforting to see her in something familiar like the car. Her appearance had certainly taken him by surprise. She'd looked so...sedate. So conservative. So unlike herself.

Ryan was disappointed to find that her apartment was as neutral as she was. He'd hoped to find signs of her passion and flair hidden here, hoped to find her living in some colorful, solar-heated building that was as unique as she was.

The four-flat building was brick with a simple layout, two apartments up, two down. Hers was upstairs and faced west.

She seemed nervous as she let him in. "I used to live downstairs, but you can see the sunset much better up here. I moved in about a month ago when it became vacant. I still haven't had time to change my driver's license records to show my new apartment number, but you probably already know that, right?"

Instead of replying, he said, "I notice your name isn't on the mailbox in the foyer."

"The kid downstairs keeps peeling it off. He peels them all off."

As she spoke, Ryan automatically checked the lock on the sliding doors leading to her balcony, which held a single sickly-looking flower in a drab pot.

She'd never had a green thumb, but that hadn't stopped her from trying. "This lock is flimsy," he noted with a frown of disapproval. "A two-year-old could open it."

Her voice was mocking as she noted, "Crime here in Fell isn't exactly on the rise."

"It is now." Spying a length of metal pipe propped in the corner, he dropped it into the slide of the doorjamb. "That's better."

Ryan turned back to the apartment. More beige. She didn't have much furniture. "What happened to that great fire-engine red beanbag chair you had?"

"I sold it at a garage sale in Chicago."

"Too bad." He had fond memories of that chair and their attempts to make love in it.

At least the couch was comfortable, although it was about three feet too short for him to sleep on, which meant he'd have to fall back on plan B—spreading his sleeping bag out on the floor. Oh well, he'd had worse assignments, but no one had ever gotten under his skin like Courtney.

"I'd like the name and phone number of your supervisor." Her voice was businesslike, contrasting the few wayward tendrils of her blond hair that had escaped the tight bun.

Ryan provided her with the information and watched her slender fingers impatiently punch out the numbers on her beige standard-issue phone. She didn't wear any nail polish. She used to have a fondness for Passionate Pink and for running her painted nails and fingertips over every inch of his torso, pausing to torment and delight in some very sensitive spots.

At the moment she seemed more interested in giving Wes Freeze a piece of her mind. "So basically you're telling me that I have no choice, that I'm legally obligated to assist the U.S. Marshals Service. But why does that mean Ryan has to stay here in my apartment. Eating my food?" A pause. "Oh, so he'll supply his own food. Is that supposed to make me feel better?" Another pause. "It's for my own protection? Well, I think this stinks!" With that she slammed the phone receiver down. "What a boondoggle. Talk about a waste of taxpayers' dollars."

He scowled at her. "Catching one of the northwest's biggest counterfeiters is not a waste of taxpayers' dollars."

"You're not going to catch them by sleeping on my couch."

"I won't be sleeping on your couch." He waited for the startled look to flash in her big brown eyes. He wasn't disappointed.

"You are *not* sleeping in my bed." She spoke slowly, emphasizing each word.

"So you've already said. Your couch is too short so I'll use the living room floor. There's a sleeping bag and air mattress out in my car."

Five minutes later he had his stuff in her compact living room, spread out from one corner to the other.

"Do you have to make such a mess?" she complained with an exasperated look. "I have company coming over this evening."

He quirked an inquisitive brow at her. "Company as in...?"

"Fred. We have a date."

"Surely you jest."

"You're the practical joker in this room," she retorted. "Not me."

The sound of her phone ringing made her jump.

"Want me to get that?" Ryan asked.

"No! I can get it myself." She grabbed for the phone.

"Courtney, it's me," said the muffled male voice.

She recognized her uncle's voice immediately. "Yes." Her cautious tone alerted her uncle.

"Someone is with you?"

"That's right. How are things?" To Ryan she mouthed, "It's a girlfriend of mine." The answer seemed to satisfy him because he started unzipping his sleeping bag, but he stayed well within earshot.

"Things they are complicated."

"I heard."

"Then you have heard that the Zopo brothers, they are bad people. They were not pleased to hear I might be testifying against them." Anton's Czech accent was more pronounced than usual, a sure sign he was upset. "There is so much to tell you, but I will be brief. Your phone might be tipped. No, that is not right. Tapped, right?"

"Right."

"I did not do wrong. I am no counterfeiter."

"I know that."

"The Zopos own the print shop." He spoke rapidly now, the words spilling out. "I was good manager. I mind my own business. But then I find a box. I should not have looked, but like Pandora I did. It was filled with blank checks. Fake checks. The government want me to testify about seeing the fake checks, the Zopos say they will do bad things if I do talk. So I take off. You know I do not think government is good at doing things, like protecting me from Zopos. I need time to think.''

"I can understand that," she said carefully. "You have to do what you think is best. Call me anytime."

"You be careful of Zopos." Anton's voice reflected his concern for her. "I wanted to warn you of this. I never told them about you, but they have ears in many places. Be careful."

"I will. You, too."

"I love you, *malenka*." The line went dead.

"What was that all about?" Ryan asked.

"A girlfriend just broke up with a jerk of a man. I told her she was right to dump him. A guy who can't make a commitment isn't worth wasting her time on."

Far from being crushed by her disdain, Ryan seemed amused. "Speaking from personal experience were you?"

"Absolutely. Not that Fred is anything like that. He's much more centered."

"*Rooted* is more the term I'd use," Ryan said. "Or *atrophied* would also apply."

She glared at him.

"What?" he demanded with feigned innocence.

"I should have expected that you'd feel threatened by a man as sure of himself as Fred."

"Me? Threatened? By Fred?" Ryan laughed. "That's a good one. For a minute there I thought you were actually serious."

"I was serious. Obviously you're not." She kicked his sleeping bag in a way that made him think she wished it was him she was kicking. That gave him hope. Because now she was acting more like the passionate woman he'd known in Chicago and not the uptight conservative clone she'd been when he'd first walked in the bank.

"I see you've still got a temper," he noted with approval.

"If I really still had a temper, you'd have a black eye." Her cheeks glowed with anger. "You seem bent on butting into my life and messing everything up. You've got your belongings strewn all over my living room."

He grinned. Yep, this was more like the Courtney he'd known. And lusted after. And bedded. All he had to do was keep pushing her buttons and he'd get the results he wanted. "Sorry about that, sis."

"Don't push your luck, buster." The sound of her bedroom door slamming made his grin widen. He was getting to her all right. Yes, siree.

RYAN WAS THUMBING through one of her magazines when Courtney finally sashayed out of her bedroom thirty minutes later. She'd changed out of her beige suit into beige chinos and a preppie white oxford shirt. Her hair was the only untamed thing about her. She'd undone it and let it fall loose.

"I'm glad you didn't cut your hair." The words slipped from his lips.

She didn't verbally acknowledge his comment, but she did grab for a hair barrette from the coffee table and gather her hair back into a more restrained ponytail.

Before Ryan could annoy her some more, Fred arrived.

"You look charming." Putting his arm around Courtney, he kissed her. It was all Ryan could do not to grab the little wimp and punch his lights out. "Are you ready?"

"We're both ready," Ryan replied even though the question was directed to Courtney. "I figured you wouldn't mind my tagging along."

"I do mind." Courtney glared at him.

Ryan flashed her a warning look. "You're such a kidder, sis." He draped an arm around her shoulders, thereby nudging Fred aside.

Courtney stepped on Ryan's toes. But it was like a mosquito landing on a rhino, for all the effect her dainty gym shoes had on his heavy-duty running shoes.

Ryan grinned at her while jauntily inquiring, "Where are we all off to this evening?"

"The drive-in." Courtney wiggled away from him to stand closer to Fred and glare at Ryan. "Not your cup of tea."

"I love drive-ins," Ryan insisted. "Surely you remember that about me, sis." Turning his attention to the geeky banker, Ryan added, "So, Frank, have you met the rest of Courtney's family or am I the first?"

"His name is Fred!" Courtney growled.

"Right." Ryan's nod was dismissive rather than at all apologetic.

"I only met her uncle once," Fred replied.

"Ah, good old uncle Anton." Ryan's attention returned to the case. "When did you meet him?"

"Last Christmas."

"And that was the last time you saw or heard from him?"

Fred nodded. "That's right."

"So what did you think of him?" Ryan asked again.

"He seemed like a nice gentleman."

Nice? Try wily as a coyote. Ryan tapped down his anger at being taken for a fool by Courtney's uncle.

"And what did Anton think of you, Fred?"

"I'm sure I don't know."

"He liked Fred very much," Courtney insisted.

For some reason Ryan doubted that. He had a hard time seeing the fun-loving Anton getting along with the uptight Fred. In the old days Courtney used to brag that she'd gotten her love for life from her uncle.

In those days, Anton had had a bohemian approach to things. Except his niece. Anton had been surprisingly old-fashioned about her. And as protective as hell. Which is why Ryan was certain that Anton would contact Courtney, if for no other reason than to assure himself of her safety. As soon as he called, they'd have him, provided he stayed on the line long enough for the tap on her phone to work, which shouldn't be a problem given Anton's normal long-windedness.

"So Anton liked you, Fred. That's nice to hear." Ryan's voice made it clear that he thought the opposite.

"Yes, well...if we don't leave now we'll be late for the movie," Fred said with a worried look at his expensive watch.

"If you must come with us, you can follow us in your car," Courtney told Ryan.

"I thought we'd carpool. Conserve gasoline, you know." Seeing the look on her face, Ryan relented. "Then again, maybe I should just follow you in my car."

ONCE SHE WAS SEATED in the passenger seat of Fred's silver luxury car and they were on their way to the drive-in, he noted, "Your half brother seems possessive of you. Why haven't you ever mentioned him before?"

"We've been out of touch for a few years."

"Really?" Fred pulled to a stop at the only traffic light in Fell, which always seemed to turn red whenever Courtney was in the vicinity. "Why is that?"

"Um, we had a fight."

"Oh. Then why is he staying with you? Is he making a nuisance of himself?"

Of course Ryan was making a nuisance of himself but she couldn't tell Fred that.

"If he is," Fred added, patting her knee, "I'll give him the old heave-ho."

That's all she'd need, Fred and Ryan in a rumble. She patted Fred's hand before returning it to the steering wheel. "There's no need. My brother is a little strange, but he's harmless."

"You're sure?"

"I can handle Ryan," she said, praying her words would not come back to haunt her.

The drive-in, on the southern edge of town, was playing an action-packed movie that was probably already in the video stores in Portland. But life was slower here in Fell.

Ryan pulled up right behind them as they took the turnoff into the theater. She'd hoped that it would be crowded, forcing Ryan to park farther away, but luck wasn't going her way. He parked in the space next to theirs and then had the audacity to wave at her.

Actually Ryan had to wave or risk giving in to the temptation to wring Fred's neck. The guy drove a car that Ryan had lusted after for the past two years. And he had his arm draped around the woman Ryan had… The woman he'd what? Had incredible sex with? Had lived with? Had let go? Had haunted his memory ever since?

Ryan wasn't able to put a label on Courtney. And at the moment, he wasn't able to get within ten feet of her.

He had the feeling she was deliberately snuggling up to Fred in the front seat. He hoped the car had a stick shift that would get in their way. He hoped this case didn't drive him crazy before he caught up with Anton. And he hoped that he'd get to kiss Courtney at least once before this was all over.

THE COMING ATTRACTIONS were rolling while the tiny speaker attached to the window provided the sound.

The click of the car's back door opening made Courtney jump and spill her box of popcorn in her lap.

"Hi, there," Ryan said as he slid into the back seat. "I just visited the concession stand and picked up more than I can handle, so I thought I'd come on over and offer to share. " He held out a huge box of buttered popcorn between the bucket front seats. "Dig right in. Oh, look, this clip is really great. I love the part where the aliens land."

He might love the clip, but he'd never loved her. Courtney wanted to clobber him.

Then things went from bad to worse as Ryan cheerfully said, "So, Fred, exactly what are your intentions toward my sister?"

3

"DON'T ANSWER THAT question, Fred," Courtney ordered, her voice trembling with anger. "Ryan is an inveterate practical joker and this is just another example of him kidding around."

"Hey, I was just looking out for your best interests," Ryan maintained.

"I know exactly what you were doing." How could she not, when he'd surreptitiously slid his hand around the side of the seat near the door to caress her shoulder. "And I want you to stop it right now."

Fred cleared his throat. "Ahem, the movie has started."

"You're right. The movie has started. So be quiet, Ryan." She covertly batted his hand away.

"Yes, ma'am." Laughter was evident in his voice.

She wished she could also order Ryan to keep his hands to himself, but there was no way she could do that with Fred sitting beside her. She couldn't even give Ryan a reprimanding look because it was dark in the car's interior, which allowed Ryan to get into all kinds of mischief.

While Fred sedately held her left hand, Ryan teased her right arm from the tip of her shoulder clear to her inner wrist, each feathery brush of his fingertips burn-

ing right through the cotton of her shirt. She tried
ignoring him, but when Ryan gently tugged on the
back of her collar in order to steal secret caresses
across the sensitive nape of her neck, she knew she
was in deep trouble. Time was supposed to heal
wounds; you'd think it would also dilute the powerful
impact of Ryan's touch.

But, no. Instead it was as if she were split down
the middle, with the sensible side of her leaning closer
to Fred while her wild side responded to Ryan's
temptation.

Ryan's warm thumb brushed her earlobe. "Are you
cold?" Fred asked in concern as he saw her shiver.

"I'm fine." Courtney's voice was unsteady, just
like her heartbeat as Ryan rubbed a strand of her hair
between his fingers.

"You seem to be shivering," Fred said.

"The movie is scaring me." The movie…and her
reaction to Ryan's touch. She shouldn't be this susceptible, not after all this time. What was wrong with
her? Whatever it was, she needed to get it fixed
pronto.

Was Ryan fingering her bra strap? Trying to slide
it off her shoulder? Outraged, she captured his wan-
dering fingers and pinched them. Muffled laughter
from the back told her she'd finally gotten his attention, but he obviously still wasn't taking her seriously.

Sure enough, seconds later his fingers traced the
curve of her ear. Had he remembered that she'd been
particularly susceptible to being touched there? Did
he know how she'd used to melt when he'd lazily
swirl his fingertips over her skin that way?

He knew. He remembered. She could tell by the confidence of his touch. He was doing this deliberately to drive her crazy.

She wouldn't let him. She refused to allow herself to fall back into bad habits. And she was not about to give Ryan the upper hand. Or the lower one, either.

She cautiously turned her head toward the passenger door, away from Fred and toward Ryan's seductive teasing. When she felt the brush of his fingers across her lips, for a moment, the memories of his touch were so strongly resurrected in her soul that she almost gave in.

This isn't about you. It's about me. About my future.

Ryan's words replayed in her mind, snapping her out of her Ryan-induced trance. Even now, this wasn't about her, it was about Ryan and his job as a U.S. Marshal. He'd do anything to recapture her uncle. Including seduce her.

His index finger strayed to her parted lips. A second later she snapped her teeth down on his wayward digit and bit him. His muffled exclamation told her that this time she'd not only gotten his attention, but was being taken seriously.

"You okay back there?" Fred asked.

"Just dandy." Just randy was closer to the truth, Ryan thought to himself ruefully. What had started out as a way of teasing Courtney had ended up as a way of driving him nuts. He was as wound up and hard as a teenager. He'd meant to test Courtney's responsiveness, but instead had tested his own self-restraint and found it disturbingly rocky.

He had a job to do here, as he'd told her any number of times. And if seducing Courtney, or playing on their former relationship would speed up the process of tracking down Anton, then so be it. He hadn't gone looking for trouble, hadn't volunteered for this job. He was just a law enforcement official obeying a direct command.

Upon further reflection Ryan decided that this mess was actually more Anton's fault than his. If the older man had just stayed put, Courtney and Ryan wouldn't be caught up in this mess.

There was a lot at stake here. The counterfeiting case. Ryan's reputation. Anton's safety. Courtney's safety.

Ryan didn't want Courtney getting hurt. He doubted she truly realized the seriousness of the situation. She'd never been one to look on the dark side of life. Her rose-colored glasses had been firmly perched atop her adorable nose. At least that's the way the Courtney he'd known in Chicago had been.

This new Courtney had him confused. Until he'd touched her. Then the old flare of physical recognition and passion had immediately come to life. He hadn't been sure it would. He'd just been testing the waters, so to speak. He hadn't intended getting inundated with a tidal wave himself.

Ryan had known he wouldn't be the best man for this case. He'd known she wouldn't be pleased at his reappearance in her life. He *hadn't* known she'd be involved with a pencil-pushing wimp.

But that didn't change things, because now that Ryan was here, he didn't trust the job of protecting

her to anyone else. Even if it meant protecting her
from herself.

"DID YOU SEE THAT? She bit him!" Muriel sounded
deeply offended as she paced across the speaker attached to the car window.

"They have the volume turned up much too loud
on this thing," Betty stated from the other side of the
voice box.

"You can see the movie better from up here." Hattie's voice floated down to them from the car roof.

"We don't have time to be watching movies," Muriel retorted impatiently. "We've got work to do."

"Ryan is *your* charge," Hattie reminded her. "I'm
just here to help you out, sort of in an advisory ca-
pacity."

"Then advise, Miss Smarty-pants."

Hattie leaned over the edge of the car roof to pro-
claim, "My advice is to stop wearing that khaki vest,
Muriel. It doesn't do you justice. Makes you look a
little jaundiced. I keep offering to give you a makeover. After all, I did a pretty good job on Heather in
our first assignment."

"I don't want a makeover!" Muriel sounded ready
to chew nails. "I want some suggestions on dealing
with Ryan and Courtney. She's dating Fred. At least
Heather wasn't dating anyone else."

Hattie sniffed. "Dating doesn't mean Courtney
loves him."

"She certainly doesn't act like she loves Ryan,"
Muriel noted tartly. "She looks ready to rip his heart
out."

"Well, he does have some lost ground to make up for," Hattie admitted. "He did break her heart back in Chicago. You can't blame her if she isn't real eager to give him a second chance."

Muriel's expression darkened. "Maybe it would be better if I got Fred out of the picture."

"Absolutely not." Hattie stood on the car roof with hands on her hips as she glared down at her siblings. "My stars, you know how much more complicated things got when we tried to interfere with Jason and Heather. As it is, we've prompted that dear man Anton to go into hiding in order to get Ryan involved."

"He's involved with the case," Betty amended. "Not with Courtney."

Hattie clutched her hat as a sudden gust of wind picked up. "We just need to give it time."

"We don't have tons of that," Muriel declared. "We can't keep the Zopos at bay forever. We've been able to sabotage their efforts so far by messing up their computer search, but doing that kind of stuff is a little outside of our field."

"Speak for yourself," Betty declared. "I for one am a big fan of mysteries." With a wave of her magic wand she added a Columbo-style tan raincoat over her T-shirt and denim skirt. "And this case has all the makings of a good one." She rubbed her hands in anticipation, nearly setting her magic wand on fire in the process.

Muriel remained glum. "It also has the makings of a disaster."

"HOW HARD CAN IT BE?" Caesar Zopo demanded, his thin mustache quivering with emotion. His eyes were so dark they nearly blended with the pupils. Although he'd celebrated his fiftieth birthday last month, there was no sign of gray in his midnight black hair. "I give you just one job, a job I'd only have my trusted brother, blood of my blood, do. And now you come back to me and say you can't do this? You can't track down one niece?"

Brutus, younger, shorter and much heavier than his brother, bowed his head in the wake of Caesar's disapproval before trying to plead his case. "I've tried, Caesar. I need more time—"

Caesar held up his hand, his fingernails perfectly manicured and buffed to a shine. "I don't want to hear any excuses." His voice was smooth and deadly. "I just want answers. Where is this niece of Anton Leva's?"

"Somewhere in the Northwest. I think." Brutus lifted his hand to bite his thumbnail before catching himself. His brother hated his weakness, as he called it. "But the computer spit out a list of several hundred women who could be his niece. I would never have thought that many would fit the profile, but they do. I checked the program several times."

"Then check it again. And track down every woman on that list. Call them and see which one is the niece. Because we get the niece and we've got Leva. Right where we want him."

"I've been trying." Brutus tried not to whine. He knew how Caesar hated it when he whined. "I—I've been calling each name on the list, but most times I—I get answering machines...."

Caesar only held up two fingers this time. It was enough to cut off Brutus's stumbling voice. "Correct me if I'm wrong, but didn't I just inform you that I don't care to hear any further excuses?"

Brutus bowed his head. "Yes, Caesar."

"Then get the job done. Or I'll do it myself."

WHEN THE TIME CAME for Fred to say good-night at her front door, Courtney wasn't surprised that Ryan just stood there, refusing to leave them alone. She knew it would be useless asking him for some privacy. Not in the mood he was in this evening. He was hell-bent on making trouble.

Which left her with one option. Cupping Fred's face with her hands, she planted a huge kiss, a kiss that meant business, on his mouth. Then, giving Ryan a triumphant look, she sashayed into the apartment leaving a stunned Fred and a furious Ryan behind.

Once he'd collected himself enough to go inside, Ryan found Courtney standing in the middle of the living room, her arms wrapped around her waist, her toe tapping impatiently, her big brown eyes flashing angrily. "I don't believe your unmitigated gall!"

"Me?" he shot back. "What about you? You're the one who bit me. And then you actually had the nerve to kiss that pencil-pushing wimp as if you meant it."

"I did mean it. And that wimp...I mean *Fred* can offer me more than you ever could."

The expression on his face tightened. "More money you mean?"

"No." Stung, she took several steps back. "You never knew me at all, did you?"

"I knew you pretty damn well."

"My body, maybe. Not my heart. Fred can offer me the security of a commitment, which is more than you were ever willing to do. You wouldn't be here now if you hadn't been ordered to, if it didn't involve a case you were working on. So don't you dare think you can waltz into town and stir up trouble and ruin my life here. I've worked hard to create the new me—a woman who is serious and dependable."

"Why would you want to? There was nothing wrong with the woman you were in Chicago."

There obviously *had* been something wrong with her or he wouldn't have left her. But that was all water under the bridge. She'd built new bridges here, going in new directions. And she'd steamroll over any sexy U.S. Marshal who got in her way, lopsided smile or not.

She picked up his sleeping bag and tossed it to him. "Don't get too comfortable, you won't be here long."

BY THE NEXT MORNING Ryan was honestly able to say that he hadn't gotten too comfortable sleeping on her floor. But that was as much the fault of his mind—which refused to stop replaying every moment he'd ever spent with Courtney between a pair of cool sheets—as it was his body, which contributed to the problem by remaining in a state of high alert.

There was no denying that the change in her disturbed him. He wasn't sure why, but he wanted back the exuberant woman he'd known in Chicago. He re-

fused to think about what he wanted to do with her
once the original Courtney resurfaced.

He missed the old Courtney's spontaneity. That's
the way she'd always been and he wanted her that
way again. Normally he was the methodical one,
planning each step forward. Well, he wasn't about to
forget his official reason for sticking with Courtney:
keeping her safe and keeping his own job.

Before he did anything, he had to get Courtney to
trust him again. She wasn't about to reveal her uncle's
location if she was so mad at Ryan she wasn't speaking to him.

So he tried to make amends over a bowl of cornflakes, all the while remembering the wild mixtures
of kids' cereals that Courtney used to concoct when
they'd been together. In those days he'd often wished
she'd had a more mainstream taste in breakfast food.

Trying to be courteous, he attempted to come up
with a neutral topic of conversation. "How did you
end up in Fell, Oregon anyway?"

"I liked the look of it." She wasn't about to tell
him that this is where her money ran out after leaving
her last job working in a ski resort in Colorado.

"It's a strange name for a town."

She immediately defended her new hometown. "I
like it. It got its name from the first family that settled
here. They were traveling the Oregon Trail when they
tried to take a shortcut and got lost. The family's covered wagon hit a big bump in the trail and the son
fell out of the back. Miraculously he wasn't hurt. In
appreciation, they named the place Fell and set up
housekeeping."

Imagining setting up housekeeping with Courtney again had a certain amount of appeal for Ryan. They had had a lot of fun together. More than that, he'd fallen for her like he'd never fallen for a woman before, or since. But his job still stood as a wall between them getting back together, now more than ever. Yet he couldn't help thinking what it would be like having her in his life again.

"So, what are we going to do today?" he asked.

She'd hoped to attend a Little League baseball game, but didn't feel up to introducing Ryan to her friends and their children. He'd already aroused Fred's suspicions. And aroused her. "I have no idea what *you'll* be doing, but I have some errands to run and some wash to do."

"Then that's what I'll be doing."

She shot him a skeptical look. "Last I heard you didn't know one end of a washing machine from the other."

"I'll watch, not wash."

"Watch like you did last night?" she demanded.

Ryan didn't want her reminding him of last night and the kiss he'd seen her give Fred. "He's not right for you."

"Like you'd know who is right for me," she scoffed, getting up to rinse her cereal bowl in the sink.

Ryan watched her. The leggings she wore showed off her lovely long legs better than anything he'd seen her dressed in so far. Her T-shirt was loose and baggy. She'd probably chosen it to hide her figure, but it only made him long to slip his hands beneath it and feel her soft skin, hold her breasts in the palms of his hands.

"This act of yours is bound to ricochet back on you, you know," Ryan murmured.

His words made her nervous. "What act?" *Did he suspect that it was Anton, not a girlfriend, who'd phoned her last night?*

"This act that you're a beige woman with neutral furniture."

"You're not making any sense. You've been here less than twenty-four hours and already you're incoherent." She stole a quick glance in his direction, noticing that he'd changed his T-shirt beneath the flannel shirt. Today it was navy blue instead of white.

He still looked entirely too good for comfort. You'd think that spending the night in a sleeping bag on her living room floor would make him look a little worse for wear. His tousled hair and bedroom eyes were sexier than ever. Her fingers twitched with the temptation to comb through his hair. Curses. "How long do you think this setup can last?"

"However long it takes to catch Anton. You could try helping me instead of fighting me and maybe we'd get this matter solved faster. Unless you enjoy having me around?" he suggested with feigned hopefulness.

She stopped her busywork tidying the kitchen and faced him, obviously eager to help him on his way. "What do you want to know?"

"Everything you know about your uncle."

"I've known my uncle since I was a little girl," she said. "There's no way I can tell you everything in a few minutes."

Ryan made himself more comfortable in the kitchen chair, leaning it back on two legs while lazily remarking, "Take your time."

"So that you can try to trip me up into revealing something I shouldn't?"

"What do you have to hide?"

The fact that Anton had called her. The fact that he had no intention of turning himself in to the authorities, authorities he felt were not capable of protecting him.

Maybe if she explained that to Ryan... "You have to understand something about my uncle. He has good reason to distrust government agents."

"He had no reason to distrust me."

"So you were the one who was in charge of this mess. I knew it!"

Ryan thunked the chair back on all four of its legs, irritation evident in both his body language and his voice. "I trusted your uncle to behave himself without supervision in the bathroom for ten minutes. He crawled out of the damn window. I still don't know how he managed that, it wasn't big enough to spit through."

Courtney smiled with satisfaction, pleased at how annoyed Ryan was. "It's in his blood. His parents were in the circus. He's something of a contortionist."

"You don't have to sound so proud of it. He did something very stupid and dangerous, not to mention illegal. He's been subpoenaed to testify in the case against the Zopos."

"Given his experience in communist Czechoslovakia, he doesn't trust anyone wearing a uniform. That includes you."

"I don't wear a uniform." Ryan tugged on his flannel shirt to reiterate that fact.

Courtney refused to get distracted by his sexy body. "That's a technicality. He doesn't trust a government bureaucracy to take care of him."

"But you could convince him to trust me."

"How can I do that when I don't trust you myself?"

Her words angered him. "You were the one who walked out on our relationship."

"Only after you made it clear that you had no room for me in your future."

"It wasn't like that," he denied.

"It most certainly was. And I don't aim on making the same mistake twice."

"Is that why you're hanging out with Fred the friendly banker?" Ryan growled.

"We already had this discussion last night." Grabbing a towel, she wiped down a kitchen counter that was already spotless. It was amazing she didn't erase the gold flecks in the Formica, so diligently was she scrubbing.

"I can't believe how you kowtowed to him."

Turning to face him, she growled, "I do not kowtow to anyone!" She wished she had a dirty dish sponge to throw at him.

"You were practically simpering."

Taking a deep breath, she regained control of her anger. "I know what you're trying to do here. You're trying to pick a fight with me, hoping I'll say something I shouldn't.''

''I'm hoping to find the woman who made love with a passionate intensity that blew my mind. The woman who loved to lick raindrops from her face in a storm and belt out Everly Brothers' hits in the shower so loudly you could hear her a block away.'' The shower had been quiet this morning. There had no been verses of ''Bye Bye Love'' or ''Wake Up Little Susie.'' And that upset him more than he'd thought. ''The woman who defied the odds and dared to do her own thing.''

''I told you,'' she said flatly. ''That woman is gone.''

''Convince me.'' In a flash, Ryan was on his feet and at her side. Snaring her in his arms, he kissed her.

4

FROZEN. She'd been frozen in a block of ice all these years and Ryan was applying a blowtorch to set her free. It sounded painful, but it sure didn't feel that way. It felt incredible. Both liberating and frustrating. He was teasing her with the tip of his devilish tongue, coaxing her to part her lips.

When she did, he rewarded her by intensifying the already heated kiss to a new level of thermal dynamics. Merging mouths and darting tongues. Slick, wet and hot. Luscious and molten.

Her breasts were tightly pressed up against his chest, her hands resting above his racing heart. She felt the beat pounding into her open palms. Ryan's large hand easily encompassed the back of her neck, holding her in place while he hungrily devoured her mouth.

She wasn't going anywhere. She couldn't get enough of him.

Rampant need coursed through her, keeping time with her throbbing heartbeat.

Closer. She needed to get closer.

Her hands slid down his torso, registering the softness of his flannel shirt, measuring the warmth of his body beneath the layers of clothing. She curled her fingers into the belt loop of his jeans, preparing to tug him closer as she'd done so often in the past.

This time her hands brushed against something foreign. Stunned, she pulled herself out of his arms. "You're wearing a gun."

"That's right." His voice was husky with passion even if his inflection was mocking as he added, "It would be pretty hard to protect you with a slingshot."

He'd been right. The passionate woman Courtney had once been was still there, beneath the beige exterior. But what had he proved?

That he still wanted her more than he'd ever wanted another woman in his entire life? That her mouth was the stuff poets write about? That her tongue could bring him to the point of no return and make him want more?

All of the above were true. The question was, what was he going to do about it?

Courtney looked as if she were grappling with some questions of her own. But when she spoke it was to issue an ultimatum. "Keep your kisses and your guns to yourself."

Ryan made one more attempt. "This Fred guy is all wrong for you, can't you see that?"

Lifting her chin, she got a stubborn look on her face. "No, I can't see that."

"He'll kill your spirit."

"Impossible." Courtney delivered the final shot. "Because you already accomplished that yourself back in Chicago."

"AH, THAT WENT WELL," Muriel said with satisfaction as she perched atop the refrigerator in Courtney's kitchen. "They're finally kissing. What?" she added as Hattie shook her head in dismay, the droopy brim of her lime hat flopping against her forehead.

"Didn't you hear what she said? She said he killed her spirit." Hattie spoke the words with great drama and sorrow.

Muriel shrugged. "She was exaggerating."

Hattie's look was reproachful. "She's still hurting."

"Well, she should get over it!" Muriel's impatience clearly showed on her face and in the way she ran her fingers through her hair, restoring the short white strands to their customary bushy look. "This is no time to get emotional. I swear, humans are impossible. Next time I want to work with animals. Cats and dogs. Horses. They've got to have more sense than humans."

"Now you're starting to sound like Betty."

Muriel glared at Hattie. "There's no need to be insulting."

"I heard that," Betty interjected, having just appeared at their side in a burst of cosmic energy. She was still wearing the same Columbo-style baggy raincoat that had been her attire since the drive-in movie the night before. "And while you two were here squabbling amongst yourselves, I paid the Zopo brothers a little visit to check things out. That glitch we put in their computer is still messing things up nicely."

Muriel's frown deepened. "Hey, I'm as much a mystery fan as the next fairy godmother, but sabotaging criminals is really beyond our realm of expertise.''

"We don't actually have a realm of expertise yet," Hattie felt compelled to say. "We're still working on that."

"For petunia's sake, I've seen every episode of 'Murder, She Wrote' and 'Columbo' and read every case of Sherlock Holmes," Betty bragged, throwing back her shoulders with confident bravado. "I think it's safe to say that I'm an expert on mysteries and that I have a surplus of deductive reasoning myself.

"We need to concentrate on the present." She continued. "We have a delicate balancing act to perform here, between uniting Ryan with his soul mate and protecting all involved from the Zopo brothers."

"We've never been good at balancing things. That's how we got into trouble in the first place," Muriel reminded her. "You couldn't balance your jelly jar of fairy dust."

"*I* wasn't the one who spilled my dust," Betty immediately denied. "*You* were the one who spilled yours from that weird container. I sneezed on my fairy dust."

"Listen, I hate to keep harping on this," Hattie interrupted while meticulously fussing with the puffy sleeves on her lime-colored silk chiffon dress, "but a petri dish is simply not an appropriate place for a fairy godmother to keep her fairy dust, Muriel. And that vest you're always wearing isn't really appropriate, either. I've told you again and again, the color completely washes out your complexion—especially up here on this atrocious avocado green refrigerator."

Hattie shuddered. "You'd look much better in something like this—" With a wave of her magic wand, Hattie turned Muriel's beloved khaki photographer's vest a dainty periwinkle blue. "That's much better."

Muriel was not amused. "It is not. I look like a blue blimp!" With a sharp whisk of her wand, she restored her vest to its original color.

"You do not look like a blimp." *Zap,* the vest was periwinkle blue again. "You look nice. Feminine and dainty."

"I hate dainty and feminine." Muriel's magic wand was turning crimson red with fury as she brandished it like an avenging knight. "If you like this stupid color so much, *you* wear it."

Hattie tried to duck as a bolt of the dreaded khaki color scored a direct hit on her, drenching not only her dress, but her hair, her hat, even her nails. Appalled, she instantly shot back a flash of periwinkle as she and Muriel engaged in a veritable chromatic war. She might be soaked, in garish tints that only magic could make, but she was pleased to see that Muriel was faring no better.

It was left to Betty to finally lay down the law, using her own powers to forcibly remove her dueling sisters' magic wands.

Propping her hands on her hips, she gave them each an exasperated look before adding her own fashion observations. "I hear that the tie-dyed look of the sixties is coming back," she mused. Both Muriel and Hattie had splotches of every color of the rainbow splattered across their clothing and their faces. "It would serve you both right if I left you this way for a decade or two.''

After they looked suitably repentant, Betty restored them to order with a flourish of her wand, while giving a bit of big sisterly advice in her drill sergeant voice. ''Conserve your energy for the important stuff. I have a feeling we're going to need it to keep one step ahead of the Zopo brothers.''

STANDING IN HIS brother's well-appointed office, with a Wagner opera playing in the background, Brutus rubbed his perspiring palms on his baggy trousers before speaking. ''I found someone who said he's sure he heard Anton talking about his niece and that she's here in Oregon.''

Caesar's eyebrow rose. ''Did you get her name yet?''

''Not exactly.'' Brutus shifted uncomfortably. ''He thought it ended in *ie* or *y*. Annie or Mary or Cathy or Stacy—''

Caesar slashed his elegant hand through the air, slicing through Brutus's words. ''Or a thousand other options. Do you know how many girls' names end in *ie* or *y?*''

''No.'' Brutus blinked uncertainly. ''Did you want me to look into that?''

''No, I don't want you to look into that!'' Caesar roared, standing up to pound his clenched fist on his mahogany desktop. ''I want you to find Leva's precious niece and I want you to bring her to me in the next twenty-four hours or else. Now get out of here.''

Brutus went. He had no stomach for tension.

Twenty-four hours. He'd have to stay at the computer all night. Popping an antacid, he decided it was time to call in some help for this job. But he didn't want Caesar finding out, didn't want him thinking he couldn't take care of things himself. Which meant he'd have to call in someone outside of their own circle.

The only person he knew was Stella, the woman he'd been courting unbeknownst to Caesar. She was the sweetest woman on the face of the earth, a shy and dainty flower. Those rumors of her being a con woman were vicious lies. When Brutus had fibbed and told her he was an investment manager, she'd looked at him with awe.

Caesar never looked at him with awe. Actually, no one ever had. Not until Stella.

So when she'd begged him to help Jimbo, her beloved younger brother, by giving him a job, Brutus hadn't been able to refuse. Jimbo swore he'd do whatever Brutus needed him to do, no questions asked. Which meant that Jimbo might be just the guy to help Brutus out—by capturing Courtney for him as soon as Brutus located her. It would be nice to have someone else doing some of the grunt work for a change.

AN HOUR AFTER Ryan kissed her, Courtney was still trying to recover. Since the cataclysmic event she'd been holed up in her room, but the space was tiny and starting to make her claustrophobic. Besides, she had things to do, dirty clothes to wash, groceries to buy. There was no food left in the house.

But if she had no food, then neither did Ryan. It

would serve him right if he starved. Then she remembered a small detail—his stash of junk food. She'd seen the pile of chips and cookies in his duffel bag. He probably had enough to last him until winter.

And the worst thing was that Courtney knew that there was no getting away from him, not unless she wanted to try to wiggle out a window the way her uncle had. She might have ventured it at one point in her past, but not now. It wasn't the responsible thing to do.

Of course, Ryan would argue that not telling him everything about her uncle wasn't responsible, either. But she owed her first loyalty to Anton. Maybe she should hire him a good lawyer, someone to do Perry Mason proud, although how she'd pay for it she wasn't sure. And she didn't actually know much about the details of her uncle's case. She needed to talk with Anton again and get more information. As it was, she had only the barest of facts.

If you're facing facts, her inner voice taunted, *then how about the facts dealing with you and Ryan? Like the way you melted in his arms.*

He'd caught her by surprise. That's what had happened. She'd been momentarily weak, overcome by the nostalgia of old memories.

Yeah, right.

Drat. She couldn't even lie to herself worth spit. How was she supposed to lie to Ryan? There was no way she could let him see the truth, that he'd gotten to her. That being the case, there was still no way he could kiss information out of her. Was there?

It might be fun for him to try, though.

Curses, there was her wild side again, trying to stir up trouble. She needed to be sensible here, to be cautious, to be distant.

At this very moment, Ryan was probably sitting in her living room, sprawled across her couch, watching her TV and patting himself on the back for having gotten to her. The image was enough to get her moving again.

As she stuffed her dirty clothes into a laundry bag, Courtney ruthlessly stuffed thoughts of Ryan into a locked corner of her mind.

Sure enough, he was watching her TV when she opened her bedroom door. "Laundry room," she said curtly. "Downstairs." Marching across the room was made somewhat more difficult by the fact that she had to sidestep his duffel and sleeping bag.

She didn't wait to see if he was following her as she grabbed her keys and headed to the locked laundry facilities in the building's basement.

Ryan's hand shot out as she went to flip on the light switch downstairs. "Let me check it out first."

It didn't take him long to do so, since the room was postage-stamp-size. "Okay, you can come on in now."

"Thank you so much." Her sarcasm was lost on him. Within seconds she realized how his presence filled the tiny area.

Filled it, heck, he commandeered it, making it his own. She had the definite feeling he'd like to do the same to her. Commandeer her, make her do his bidding.

Not even bothering to sort through the laundry, she

dumped it all in one load, praying there was nothing red in there to discolor the rest of the clothes. Stuffing in quarters, she set the machine and tried to make a quick getaway.

"Aren't you forgetting something?" Ryan asked, barring her way.

She eyed him suspiciously. "If you think I'm kissing you to get out of here, you're crazy."

"I hadn't thought of that." His grin was teasing. "I meant you forgot to put in any laundry detergent."

"Since when have you become Suzie Homemaker?" she muttered, even as she returned to the washer.

"Hey, I haven't forgotten that time I used dishwashing liquid instead of laundry soap."

She smiled at the memory of bubbles cascading out of their laundry room in Chicago. "I still say that would have worked if you'd just gotten the proportions right."

"Not my strong suit."

"I know." If he'd gotten the proportions right in their relationship it would have worked, too. But he'd gone overboard with his independence and his career.

But that didn't bear thinking about. After sprinkling in a handful of detergent, she reset the machine and hightailed it back upstairs.

Vacuuming made her feel better. She went at it like a woman possessed. Which, of course, she was. Possessed by the forbidden memory of his kiss, of his mouth covering hers, of his tongue swirling over hers.

Distracted as she was, she nearly sucked up her single indoor houseplant, a hardy philodendron that had survived all her moves westward. Ryan's reaction to her whirlwind cleaning was to sit on her couch and lift his feet out of her way as she vigorously steered the cleaning appliance in his direction. Finally he had enough. Pulling the plug, he said, "We have to talk."

Anticipating trouble, she wrapped her arms around her middle to calm her jittery stomach before she met the mocking glint in his hazel eyes head-on. "I refuse to discuss what happened this morning."

"I meant about your uncle."

Of course about her uncle. Because that was work. Anton's escape was a blot, no doubt, on Ryan's record. She knew that any move on his part to try to seduce her was simply his way of trying to get the job done.

Taking a small black notebook out of the pocket of his flannel shirt, Ryan fixed her with an I-mean-business stare. "I'll need the name of all your uncle's friends, people he might contact." Seeing the stubborn set of her chin, he added, "There is such a thing as obstruction of justice, you know. You can't help Anton if you're behind bars."

That took some of the wind out of her sails as she sank to the couch and tried not to show her jumpy emotions. "My uncle doesn't have any close friends. He has lots of acquaintances, but no one that knows him well."

"Besides you."

"Besides me," she confirmed.

"So give me the name of his acquaintances."

She listed all the ones she was familiar with because she was sure her uncle wouldn't be contacting any of them.

"I'm glad to see you're cooperating." Ryan ruined it by adding, "Finally."

She wanted to smack him. Instead, she headed back to the laundry room to shift her clothes from the washer to the dryer.

Ryan trailed after her, watching her every move. His presence was even more overwhelming in the close confines. Moving blindly, she bent over to reach into the washer's deep tub to grab her mangled-looking wet clothes, all the while aware that Ryan was probably eying her derriere. She'd gained some weight since they'd been together in Chicago, and at that moment it felt as if it had all settled in her bottom and thighs.

The beige slacks she'd worn before were baggy enough to hide that fact, but today she was wearing leggings which hid little. Yanking open the front-loading dryer door, she tossed her clothes inside and started jabbing the required change into the machine.

"You forgot something." Ryan's teasing voice should have warned her that whatever he held in his hands would be incriminating. It was. Her lacy ecru panties looked even more delicate against his masculine hand. "Won't you be needing these?"

She grabbed them from him and tossed the traitorous item of clothing into the dryer. It would serve it right if it shrank in the dryer.

As Ryan watched her, he couldn't get over how much he wanted to see her in those lacy panties and nothing else. He wanted to slowly peel them from her body, a body that had ripened in all the right places. Courtney might be trying to turn her life into a staid regimentation but beneath it all were passionate signs that the old Courtney was alive and kicking...and kissing him back.

An instant later Ryan's teasing look turned grim as someone entered the tiny laundry room. In his line of work, Ryan had to be prepared for the worst. Felons weren't usually the most polite element of society. And the guy who'd just walked in on them looked as mean and ornery as any of the scumbags Ryan had brought in on a warrant.

The guy was huge. His hair was greased back in a ponytail, his auburn beard was bushy, and his black T-shirt had the logo of a Portland motorcycle gang. Most important, he was carrying a baseball bat, smacking it against his hand with menace as he rushed toward Courtney.

Ryan, his body language conveying raw aggression, stopped the intruder in his tracks. "Back off!"

Ryan had the guy up against the basement wall ready to frisk him before Courtney could blink. Or speak.

She quickly recovered. "Ryan, that's my neighbor you're getting personal with! He's a friend. His name is Red."

"This bozo bothering you?" Red demanded, even as he straightened from the undignified position Ryan held him in.

"This bozo is named Ryan. I'm sorry he grabbed you like that."

Red gave Ryan a leery look. "He do that kind of thing very often?"

Ryan knew when his masculinity was being questioned. So did Courtney. He could tell by her grin as she replied, "I couldn't say. I haven't seen him in a long time. I'm sorry I missed your baseball game this afternoon, Red. Did your kids' team win?"

Red shook his head. "Not this time. But we all went out for ice cream afterward, so they didn't seem to take it too hard."

"Red is a real gem." Courtney beamed, making Ryan wish she'd look at him that way. "He does so much for underprivileged kids, including coaching a Little League team."

"Sorry about the misunderstanding," Ryan apologized gruffly. "I thought you might be a threat to Courtney's safety."

"Red is my protector." Courtney linked her arm through Red's while flashing Ryan a defiant look. "*He'd* never hurt me."

And what am I? Ryan thought. I'm supposed to be your protector. But he had hurt her by his behavior back in Chicago. Nor did she seem willing to forgive and forget. At least, not yet. Although she'd certainly kissed him as if she meant it.

As she made small talk with Red, Courtney could tell that Ryan was thinking about kissing her. She could see it in his eyes. The room was closing in on her.

She fled back upstairs with Ryan hot on her heels. She could practically feel his breath on the back of her neck. She couldn't take it anymore. Once they were inside her apartment, she confronted him. "Do you have to stand so close to me? Is this the way you guard the rest of your prisoners?"

"You're not a prisoner."

It felt like she was. A prisoner of her own desire for him. A desire that she couldn't, wouldn't give in to.

"Since you're staying here, dirtying half the dishes, you might as well do half the work." She knew, from living with him, that Ryan hated doing dishes. He'd immediately gotten a dishwasher when he'd moved into a building without one. "The dishes are in the sink." She pointed toward the small kitchen. "I'm going to dust in here while you do that."

At least he'd be in the next room and out of this one.

"*Dust?*" he repeated, as if it were a foreign word. "You never used to dust."

"I never used to do a lot of things I do now."

"Like what?"

"Like bake." It was the only thing she could think of on such short notice and she saw from the look on his face that it was the wrong thing to say. The man had a sweet tooth a mile long.

"Bake what?" he demanded. "Cookies? Brownies? German chocolate cake?"

"None of the above. I'm out of food. We have to go to the grocery store."

His eyes lit up with visions of desserts dancing in them. "While we're there, I'll buy the ingredients for brownies and cookies if you'll bake them."

"I bake to please myself," she informed him. "Not to please a man."

"You mean you don't bake to make an impression on Fred? He's never tasted your...goodies?"

"My goodies are none of your business," she retorted, knowing darn well he wasn't talking about food. "You'd better get those dishes done before we leave."

To give him credit, Ryan didn't protest. She spent more time eyeing him through the open archway to the kitchen than she did dusting. Even up to his elbows in soapy dishwater, he still possessed a raw masculinity that put all other guys to shame.

The timer she'd set reminded her it was time to retrieve her dried clothing from downstairs. Another trip was made, again with Ryan right behind her. She scooped the clothes from the dryer, sneaking a deep sniff of them as she did so.

Ever since she'd been a little girl, she'd loved the smell of freshly dried clothes. It reminded her of her mother. Hoping Ryan hadn't noticed her small idiosyncrasy, she dumped the clothes in a plastic basket and headed back upstairs.

She was still folding the laundry when Ryan finally finished the dishes. She was struggling to collect all four corners of a top sheet to her double bed when Ryan offered his assistance. "Here, let me help you with that."

When he stood several feet away to shake the sheet into compliance, she had no trouble. The boldly-colored sheet billowed between them. Once the wrinkles where shaken free, he came close again to hand over his two corners. Their fingers collided and tangled during the transfer. That's when things got tricky.

Because the second he touched her, shivers of irrational pleasure skipped down her spine. And with the pleasure came the yearning, along with the memories of crisp sheets and his fingers touching her. Of them rolling together in bed, intimately entwined, bare skin slick with desire as he'd arch his back and thrust into her, making her his forever.

She could tell by the heat in his hooded eyes that Ryan's memories matched her own. Her breath came in quick spurts, her lips parting. And still the connection between them grew, the images becoming more and more erotic, more and more powerful—binding her to him as surely as golden chains.

His fingers tightened on hers. His gaze shifted from her eyes to her parted lips. The sheet between them retained some heat from the dryer and reflected it back. She was already burning up, caught up in the moment.

He'd kissed her once today. He wanted to kiss her again. She could read the hunger in his eyes. She knew because she felt the same way. The taste of him was addictive. She'd never get enough. Never get enough of him. She'd loved him with everything she had. And it still hadn't been enough.

Ryan made his move, swooping down to capture her lips with his own. But she surprised him, stuffing the now crumpled sheet in his face. By the time he shoved it aside, she was safely on the other side of the room, with her car keys in hand. "I think it's time we got some fresh air."

THE FIRST THING Ryan discovered Monday morning was that the apartment building's hot water heater wasn't large enough. Last night he'd discovered that Courtney could still drive like a maniac when it suited her. And he had the feeling that his being in the car had been the motivating factor in her Evel Knievel impression.

They'd spent more time in the grocery store than he had in years. She seemed determined to stay there, rechecking each aisle, picking up every item on her list and checking the ingredients, reading the nutritional percentages as if they were the opening lines of a summer blockbuster novel. She'd refused to buy anything to bake for him, not even a brownie mix, but had instead filled up the cart with tons of healthy stuff from the natural food aisle.

She'd been trying to avoid him. He knew that. And part of him felt a tad guilty about it. The rest of him had wished they were back at her place, naked and making out on her freshly washed sheets.

This morning she still seemed intent on making him pay.

"You used up all the hot water," he complained as he joined her in the kitchen. He was wearing jeans and was still fastening the top button.

She eyed his bare chest with disapproval. "I thought you could use some cooling off."

Ryan leisurely tugged on his white T-shirt, very much aware of her gaze as he did so. He didn't get to work out much, but chasing down felons had kept him in pretty good shape. He was glad of that fact, as he noticed the passion growing in her big brown eyes. "Still mad about the fact that you kissed me back yesterday?"

She thumped the cornflakes box on the table so fiercely that its contents almost jumped out the top. "I did *not* kiss you back."

"You sure did. And I liked it. A lot."

"Is that supposed to impress me?"

He shrugged. "I was just stating a fact."

"Well, stop it. I don't want to hear anything more about that kiss." She was so rattled she grabbed a fork to eat her cereal with before realizing what she'd done and quickly switching to a spoon. "I want to know what you've done about ensuring my uncle's safety."

"There's not much I can do until he contacts you. And I know that being concerned about his safety, if he were to call in, you'd do the right thing and notify me immediately, right?"

She blinked at him guilelessly. "You mean you don't have a tap on my phone?"

"I'd rather not answer that question."

"Then I'd rather not answer your questions, either."

"Tit for tat?" His low-pitched voice was mocking. "Don't you think that's a little childish?"

"No more so than you stealing kisses when I'm not looking."

"You've been looking plenty," he murmured provocatively.

"There you go again."

"Me?" His expression was innocent. The gleam in his eyes was not. "I wasn't the one who brought up that kiss again. You seem to be fascinated by it."

"And therefore fascinated by you?"

"Why don't you tell me?"

"Forget it." She splashed milk in her cereal bowl. "Because all I'm interested in is my uncle's safety. And I don't see you doing much about it."

He wasn't about to tell her what was going on behind the scenes. He didn't trust her not to clue Anton in. He'd run a check on the names she'd given him yesterday of her uncle's acquaintances and had called most of them. None had heard from Anton.

No airline tickets had been issued in his name, either. Ryan had a hunch that Anton wasn't all that far away. And he hadn't forgotten the other man's early experience as an actor, which meant he had the know-how to change his appearance.

Ryan might not be an actor, but he knew a thing or two about changing appearances. He knew he'd done his job well by the double take Courtney gave him as he exited the bathroom a few minutes later. He'd changed clothes, and personalities to a certain extent.

She frowned at him. "Why are you wearing that strange-looking suit?"

"You don't like it?" He tugged on the baggy houndstooth jacket and equally ill-fitting waistband of the slacks.

"It isn't you."

"That's what I keep saying about your clothes," he returned with a grin.

"Forget it." She threw her hands up in the air. "Forget I said anything. It's really none of my business. Just as what I do is none of your business."

But Ryan aimed on making it his business. Which is why once they got to the bank, and Courtney was distracted by a conference with Francis, he headed for Fred's glass-enclosed office. From there he could still keep an eye on Courtney while he took care of something that needed clearing up.

Fred eyed him warily, apparently no more a fan of Ryan's new look than Courtney was. "Is there something I can do for you?"

"As a matter of fact, Fred, there is." Ryan sank into the visitor's chair with casual nonchalance. "I thought it would be best if we spoke man-to-man."

"You're not going to ask about my intentions again, are you?"

Ryan arched a brow. "That made you feel uncomfortable, did it?"

Fred's expression was filled with disapproval. "Courtney tells me you're a great kidder, but I'm not into that type of humor myself."

"Trust me," Ryan noted, "I'm not kidding about this."

"I fail to see why you're putting on this protective brother act now, after you haven't paid much attention to your sister for some period of time. She told me you two had a falling out."

That's when Ryan dropped his first bombshell. "The thing is, Fred, I'm not really Courtney's brother."

5

"YOU'RE NOT HER BROTHER?" Fred repeated, enunciating each word with careful precision.

"Nope." Ryan settled himself more comfortably in the cushy chair across from the banker, feeling much better at having told Fred the truth.

"Then who are you and why are you staying in Courtney's apartment?"

"I'm a Deputy U.S. Marshall and I'm here to protect Courtney." Ryan showed Fred his badge, which the banker looked over carefully before handing back, a somewhat dazed look on his nondescript face.

"Protect her from what?"

"From whom," Ryan corrected him. "And I'm not at liberty to give you any further details about the case."

Fred frowned at him suspiciously. "How do I know this is legitimate?"

"I work out of the district office in Portland." Reaching into the pocket of his ill-fitting suit, Ryan pulled out a card, the same one he'd shown Courtney the night before. "Here's the phone number. You're welcome to call them and confirm my assignment."

Ryan watched while Fred did just that.

"You believe me now?" Ryan asked, waiting for

Fred's nod before continuing. "Good, because I'd appreciate your cooperation with this matter."

As he'd suspected, the skinny banker puffed his chest out with self-importance. "What do you need me to do?"

"I don't want to arouse unnecessary suspicions about my presence here in the bank. Did you tell anyone that I was supposed to be Courtney's half brother?"

Fred thought a moment before replying. "No."

"Good." Ryan nodded with satisfaction. "That simplifies things. I want you to tell your employees that I'm with the government. Be deliberately vague, let them think I'm inspecting your bank and observing your procedures."

Fred appeared flushed with excitement. Jeez, Ryan thought, the guy needed to get a life. Preferably one without Courtney.

"But you won't really be inspecting the bank, right?" Fred asked, his voice quavering just a bit.

"Right. I just need to push some papers around to make it look real."

"And how long will you be protecting Courtney?" Fred asked.

"Until she's safe."

Ryan had a tap on her phone, he figured it couldn't be much longer before Anton called her. Then it was simply a matter of tracing the call to get an idea of Anton's location. There had already been one suspiciously short call, from a pay phone outside of Portland, the one that Courtney had claimed was from her girlfriend. In his experience, women talked for hours not minutes and that time was multiplied tenfold when they were upset by something, like dumping a boyfriend.

Unfortunately the damn phone tapping equipment had mysteriously malfunctioned and instead of a recording of the conversation, all they'd gotten was a bunch of garbled noise. His gut told him the call had been from Anton, and that if he called once, he'd call again. This time Ryan, and the newly repaired equipment, would be ready for him.

"So can I count on you, Fred?" Ryan shot him a guy-to-guy smile.

"Sure thing." Fred practically beamed. "I appreciate you taking me into your confidence."

"No problem."

But Ryan knew there would be a problem once Courtney found out he'd gone over her head to speak to her boss. He decided it would probably be best if he told her himself, before Fred did.

She was sitting at her desk, wearing the sedate navy blue suit that he'd wanted to unbutton the second he'd seen her in it this morning. That was the problem with her conservative work clothes. All they did was provoke in him the urge to unpeel them and reveal the colorful woman beneath, the one he'd thought would stay with him forever, the one he missed.

"What do you mean you told Fred the truth?" she demanded, her big brown eyes flashing fire.

"I told him that I'm not your brother," Ryan repeated without a smidgen of remorse. "Not even your half brother."

"You told him about my uncle?"

"I'm not allowed to discuss the case," he reminded her. "I simply said I was here for your protection. And he agreed to cooperate by telling his employees that I'm one of those government pencil pushers checking into banking procedures."

Understanding dawned as she stared at him. "That's why you're wearing that suit and those funny glasses today."

Ryan looked down at his clothing before casting a rueful look in her direction. "I thought you'd like this look, given your affection for Fred."

She didn't bite on that. "You didn't tell him we knew each other before, did you?"

"Not yet."

"Not ever," she corrected him, aware of Francis's frown in their direction. "I can't talk about this now. There are customers waiting to open accounts. We'll talk about this tonight."

"I can't wait," he drawled.

Once he'd left Courtney, Ryan headed toward his desk, not far away from hers. There Francis hovered over him with an armful of files. Courtney hoped that would keep him out of her hair for a while. She just needed to keep busy, that's all.

Her thoughts were interrupted by an elderly woman, dressed in a hot pink jogging suit, plunking herself down in the chair across from Courtney. Her hair was what Anton used to refer to as a poodle cut and it was a pinkish color that almost matched her outfit.

Courtney smiled. "May I help you?"

The woman laughed. She had a hearty laugh. "I'd

like information about opening a savings account. I want to put something aside for my favorite niece." In an undertone, the woman said, "You don't recognize me, *malenka?*"

She tried not to do a double take. "Uncle Anton?" she whispered.

"I am good actor still, yes? You did not recognize me?"

"No way." She blinked at him. "I can't believe it."

"The theater training, it has come in useful during these stressful times."

"How have you been? *Where* have you been?" Her questions tumbled out one after the other.

"I am doing well, but I can tell you no more. It is better you don't know where I am staying." Turning his head, Anton shifted his eyes toward Ryan. "You did not tell me *he* was here. He has been bothering you?"

"He's not happy about you giving him the slip," she admitted. "He told me about you shimmying out that bathroom window."

"I was not sure I could do it, but I was glad to see there is still plenty of life left in the old body after all." Anton beamed at her.

"You're not even sixty yet. But still, you could have hurt yourself making your escape that way," she scolded him.

"The Zopos, they would hurt me worse."

His words chilled her heart. "Ryan is determined to track you down. He figures you'll get in touch with me, and he's staying with me until you do." To keep up appearances, she raised her voice. "You can either open the account in your niece's name or you can have a joint account."

"He's staying with you at work?" Anton asked softly.

"And at home," she replied in a whisper. "Around the clock."

"The rogue! He has been making moves on you again, yes?"

"Forget that." She patted Anton's hand, only then noticing he was wearing nail polish. "We need to worry about you." Nibbling her bottom lip with her teeth, she tried to come up with a plan. "Maybe it would be safer if you left the state."

Anton shook his head, the pinkish wig he wore bobbing ever so slightly. "That is what they think I will do."

In an undertone, she confessed her fears to him. "They think you'll stay in touch with me and I don't want to be responsible for you getting caught. Ryan seems to think that the Zopo brothers will try to use me to get to you."

"I fear this also," Anton admitted. "But I will protect you."

"It's Ryan's job to protect me. And to bring you back to testify."

Anton shot another look in Ryan's direction. "I heard them call him flypaper, because when he catches someone they stay caught. Until me."

"Flypaper, huh?" Courtney had to admit that from the first moment she'd seen him, Ryan had caught her attention and she'd stayed caught. Until their fight in

Chicago. Then her romantic house of cards had come crashing down around her ears, breaking her ace of hearts.

Aware of the charade she had to keep playing, she smiled and opened a brochure explaining the different types of savings accounts. Holding it up, she leaned toward her uncle to whisper, "I'm worried about you. Maybe it would be best if you turned yourself in. We could make sure that you're protected properly. I worry about you being on your own."

"I must go."

To her dismay, Anton abruptly heaved himself out of the chair and with a high-pitched feminine laugh, hurried toward the exit.

There was nothing Courtney could do to stop him, to help him. Or was there? Grabbing the banking brochure, she rushed after Anton. "Ma'am, you left your papers behind."

But by the time she got outside there was no sign of her pink-haired uncle.

COURTNEY HAD A hard time concentrating for the rest of the day. And it showed in the number of typing mistakes she made entering new account information into the computer.

She kept wondering where her uncle was. If he was taking care of himself, eating properly. He seemed to get a kick out of dressing up and that made her worry that he might not be taking the danger as seriously as he should. The moment she'd suggested turning himself in, he'd taken off as if someone had lit a fire under him.

Maybe she should have waited before bringing up the subject, should have pumped him for more information about where he was hiding out. She made another typo. At this rate it would take her all day to finish this project.

Of course her concentration level wasn't helped any by Ryan's proximity. She kept experiencing flashbacks of their past, like the morning he'd taped his photo to their fridge. Beneath it was a handwritten message: "Have you seen my heart? It's been missing since I met you. You hold it in your hands."

Or there was that time he'd nursed her through the flu, going out at midnight in a cold rain to find an all-night market because she had a craving for mint chocolate chip ice cream.

Then there were the poems he'd write her. Well, limericks really. They all started with the lines "There once was a guy named Ryan, who found the girl of his dreams without tryin'...."

Along with the good times, there had been plenty of fights and lots of making up. Passions had run so high.

She couldn't bear to talk to him about his work yet, ask him why he'd acted the way he had. To do that would be tantamount to admitting that she still cared for him deeply. She was a different person now, determined to go for security instead of passion. So what if Fred didn't create fireworks inside her. At least she wouldn't get burned.

The new Courtney was buttoned-down and proper. Her wardrobe reminded her every day of her mission. No more wild adventures. No more being ruled by her heart. Maybe her problems with Ryan had been that she'd loved him too much. So when he'd done his own thing by joining the Marshals Service without telling her, she'd been devastated. This time she'd be the one who loved less in the relationship. That's the way it was with Fred.

Shortly before closing time, Courtney happened to look up from her work to see a man standing at the door to the bank. This in itself wasn't an unusual occurrence, as people came and went throughout the day. But this man was bundled up as if it were December not June.

And his face looked strange. She tried to get a better look at him, but the sunlight was shining right in her eyes. That must be what was making his features so blurred.

What really got her attention was the way he was practically pounding on the glass door with frustration as he struggled to open it.

As Jimbo yanked on the bank's door again, he cursed the damn panty hose blurring his vision. It might disguise his face but he couldn't read what was printed on the bank's door. Was it closed already? He tried looking at his dinosaur watch but he couldn't make out the time.

He pounded on the door again. Damn, why did things always go wrong for him? Just once, couldn't they work out for a change?

Brutus had told him the plan was foolproof. All he had to do was pretend to rob the bank and kidnap Courtney. She worked at the bank. The one with the door that wouldn't open.

Out of the corner of her eye, Courtney saw Ryan suddenly leap to his feet and charge toward the door, leaping around old Mrs. Albergast who came in every Monday to cash in her change. Pennies and nickels went flying as the startled elderly woman dropped her piggy bank. Ryan kept on moving toward the door and the man who was having trouble with it.

Her heart in her throat, Courtney belatedly realized that the reason she hadn't been able to see the man's face wasn't because of the bright sunlight, but because of the fact that he was wearing a pair of panty hose over his head.

A bank robber? Who hadn't known to *pull* the door open instead of pushing it?

Ryan was through the door in a flash. The would-be bank robber was on the run from Ryan.

Courtney didn't know what to do. Call the police? And tell them that a man wearing panty hose on his head had had a hard time with the door? What if it was a false alarm? What if it wasn't and Ryan got hurt? She dialed 911.

The police department was just a block away so she heard the sirens even as Ryan walked back into the bank a few minutes later, his expression one of disgust. "I lost him."

JIMBO WAS BENT OVER, gasping for breath after running faster than he'd ever run in his life. He had a bad charley horse in his leg and another in his neck, which he'd nearly broken trying to remove the damn panty hose from his head. The thing had almost strangled him and it was certainly responsible for him nearly getting caught.

He wasn't sure how the bank had known ahead of time that he was coming and had locked the doors against him. He'd been very careful not to say a word, not even when the cute girl at the grocery store had given him a strange look when he'd bought the pair of queen-size panty hose. He had slipped up and said they were for himself, but then had quickly covered his tracks by saying they were for his wife. Not that he was married. Not yet. He hoped to be someday. When he had a nest egg stashed away.

The money Brutus was paying him was supposed to supply a big part of that nest egg. Now it didn't look like he'd get the rest of his payoff. And he'd heard that the Zopo brothers didn't suffer fools lightly. Jimbo had been called a fool and much worse ever since he'd been in the second grade and the other kids had made fun of him for being slow.

His sister had always stood up for him. He hoped she'd stand up for him now. Because he had no intention of going back to that bank ever again in his entire life. If Brutus wanted the job done, he could do it himself!

6

COURTNEY HOPED no one could tell that her knees were knocking. When Ryan had rushed out the door after the bank robber, he'd taken ten years off her life. But she couldn't let that show. She had to be cool, be sensible.

"It's a good thing you were here," Courtney told Ryan, trying to hide her concern behind a facade of calm as Fell's full complement of law enforcement officials—all five of them—were now swarming the bank.

Francis joined Courtney and Ryan a moment later, having just finished calming Mrs. Albergast, who was demanding reparations for her cracked piggy bank.

"You run awfully fast for a bank inspector," Francis noted with an admiring look at Ryan.

"I work out," he modestly replied.

"I can tell." Was Francis actually simpering? Courtney blinked in disbelief. Was Francis trying to flirt with Ryan?

All of a sudden, the other woman looked years younger. Now that Courtney thought about it, she was only a few years older than Ryan and herself. It was her attitude that had always made her seem so much older.

And Ryan, drat his hide, was flirting back with her. While not simpering, he was displaying the masculine equivalent. Courtney recognized the signs. Flashes of his lopsided grin. That glint in his hazel eyes, lighting them from within. A very tempting package and one that poor Francis would be helpless to resist.

Courtney ought to know. She'd been there herself.

And she was not feeling jealous. No, no she wasn't. She was merely concerned for Francis. After all, women needed to stand together. It was their feminine duty to place warning labels on men so that the next woman in the guy's life could see what was wrong with them, label them Sold as Is and list the damage—which in Ryan's case would be an inability to commit to a relationship. He valued his work more than his relationships. Oh, she could write a book about Ryan's flaws.

The problem was, she could write a multivolume epic on his good points as well.

Her reminiscences were getting her nowhere. "I hate to interrupt," she said, "but the police have indicated that they want to speak to each of us individually. Francis, you should go first since you have seniority."

As soon as the other woman was gone, Courtney directed her attention to Ryan. Only now was it truly sinking in how much at risk he'd been by chasing after a bank robber like that. She knew Ryan had a gun. But chances were that the robber had been armed as well.

She shuddered to think what might have happened had the masked thief not had trouble with the door.

Her only way of venting her feelings, which threatened to overwhelm her, was to sock Ryan's upper arm.

"Ouch!" He shot her a look of exaggerated outrage that moved her not at all, except to notice how cute he looked.

"That robber would have hurt you far worse," she said. "Do you have any idea how much danger you put yourself in by chasing him like that?"

"It's my job," Ryan stated simply.

"I hate your job," she stated, just as simply but with more vehemence.

"So you've said."

Courtney knew this wasn't the time or place for this conversation. So she let her eyes do the talking. She hoped they didn't also convey her fears for his safety, her blind relief that he was unharmed.

Ryan was getting to her. His searching gaze was stripping away her defenses and digging into her soul. So she did what any sane woman would do. She attacked. "What were you doing with Francis?"

And like any obtuse man, he jumped to the wrong conclusion. "Are you jealous?"

"Absolutely not. But I thought your job was to keep your eyes on me, not on Francis's shirtfront."

"Meow."

"Was that your impression of Felix the Cat?" Courtney inquired with mocking sweetness. "If so, it needs more work."

"You're jealous. I can tell." Ryan's voice was rich with satisfaction as he added, "You always get this little tick at the corner of your eye when you get jealous.''

She immediately put her hand to her face. "I do not!''

He removed her hand and replaced it with his own, his fingertips barely brushing the sensitive corner of her eye. "There it goes. Tick, tick, tick. Very impressive.''

If he thought that was impressive, he should feel what her heart was doing. Thumthumthumthum—one rapid beat bumping into the next as sexual awareness shot through her system. All this because he was touching her. Every cell vibrated with excitement and recognition, while shouting for more.

It didn't help that Ryan curved his fingers so that he cupped her face. His hand was so large that his thumb brushed the opposite corner of her mouth. She felt cradled, engulfed by the magic only he could produce.

His eyes were starbursts of gold and green, alive with need and disarming passion. And then she saw his slow lopsided smile, the one that said he knew he was getting to her.

The effect was the equivalent of a bucket of cold water being dumped over her head, so quickly did she snap out of it and step away from him. She shook her head so vehemently her tight bun almost came undone. "Oh, no, you don't.''

"I know I don't.'' His husky voice slid down her spine like a lover's touch. "But I want to. With you.''

She glared at him. "Keep your hands to yourself from now on, buster.''

"I just love it when you try to sweet-talk me."

She refused to be swayed by his charm. "Keep this up and you're going to be in very hot water."

His grin turned naughty. "Keeping things up has never been a problem where you're concerned."

Frantic, she looked around them to make sure they weren't being overheard. Thankfully no one was close enough to eavesdrop. Which gave her the courage to say, "For a bank inspector, you've got a wicked mouth on you."

"So you've told me before," he murmured seductively. "Usually right after I put my mouth on your…"

She clapped her hand over the item under discussion—his naughty mouth—silencing his words but not his effect on her. She affixed him with her best "you're overdrawn and you're not getting another damn cent" bank teller's look. "Behave yourself," she ordered sternly.

She could tell he wasn't taking her seriously by the way he swirled his tongue across the heart of her palm. She should have threatened to yank his tongue out, then he'd stop toying with her, but she was distracted by the molten heat he was evoking deep within her body.

"Am I interrupting something?" Francis inquired from beside them.

Courtney jumped as if she'd just been hit by lightening and yanked her hand away from Ryan's tempting mouth.

He shared a look with her that was part conspirator, part wicked lover. "Courtney was just restraining me from speculating about the robbery." His words were directed toward Francis but his attention was completely concentrated on Courtney.

"The sheriff would like to speak to you next, Ryan," Francis said.

Tiny Picton, county sheriff, was no stranger to Ryan. He joined the sheriff in the conference room the lawman had commandeered.

Tiny was a misnomer if ever there was one—the man was six foot six and had to tip the scales in the neighborhood of 380. Even his voice was big. "Well now, boy, why is it that as soon as you show up in my jurisdiction, we start having trouble with bank robberies? This have something to do with your case?"

"You want to keep your voice down, Tiny?" Ryan requested dryly. He'd checked in with the sheriff as soon as he'd hit town. Not only as a professional courtesy, but also to pump him for information about Anton. Tiny didn't know much about Anton, who'd only come to Fell a few times to visit Courtney. The print shop Anton had managed had been in a Portland suburb so Ryan hadn't held out much hope that Tiny would have any useful information, but you never knew.

"I'm not sure if this bungled robbery has something to do with my case or not," Ryan added. "But my gut tells me it does." He then went on to give a description of the height and weight of the white male suspect as well as his attire, including the panty hose pulled over his head.

"I'm assuming he's taken that off by now," Tiny

noted. "And I'm assuming the suit currently walking in the bank entrance is FBI."

Ryan was no huge fan of the FBI, few members of the Marshals Service were. There was a definite rivalry between the two federal law agencies.

After introducing himself, Agent Charles Zamika asked Tiny, "What do we have here?"

"A bungled robbery attempt."

"Any witnesses?"

"Sure thing. A U.S. Marshal." Tiny nodded toward Ryan.

The agent frowned at them both. "You think this was done by a wanted felon on the run?"

"I doubt it," Ryan replied. "It had *amateur* written all over it."

"Then what are you doing here? The Marshals Service isn't an investigative agency." Zamika made it sound like an insult.

Ryan had run into his type before. They considered a marshal's work to be a lowly combination of bailiff and process server while the FBI tracked down the real criminals. In the considered opinion of the FBI no credit was given for fugitive arrests, only for initial arrests.

It wasn't all that long ago that the two agencies had been involved in turf wars regarding who was responsible for capturing high-profile federal fugitives. Ryan wasn't about to get embroiled in the same thing on a smaller level here in Fell. He wasn't about to tell Agent Zamika any more than he had to. Releasing information on a need-to-know basis was too deeply ingrained in him to change now.

The agent, sensing that Ryan was holding back, became hostile. "Attempted robbery is a serious offense. If one of your Witness Security people has perpetrated a crime, they have to be hauled in, the same as the rest of the population."

"This has nothing to do with the Witness Security Program."

"Like you'd tell me if it did."

"You know the rules as well as I do." Ryan continued to keep his voice even, but it was requiring more and more effort. "If a protected witness commits a crime, they have to face the same punishment as anyone else."

"Most of the people in that program are criminals who copped a plea to get out of doing time."

Ryan gritted his teeth. "Like I said, I'm not involved in that program. I'm pursuing a subpoenaed witness."

"It's pretty sad when you guys can't even keep track of a witness before the trial." Zamika gave him superior look.

Ryan gritted his teeth even harder and reminded himself that throttling an FBI agent would be frowned upon by his boss. Although, come to think of it, Wes had never been a big fan of the suits with their fancy law degrees or CPA's.

"So you think that this robbery attempt was someone's way of trying to make a grab for the witness's niece? I'll check it out," Zamika said.

"Keep her name out of it," Ryan ordered curtly. "I don't want the wrong people finding out where she is."

"If your theory is correct, it sounds like they already have."

"Maybe I'm just being paranoid."

"And maybe you're right." Zamika said the words reluctantly. "I've got an evidence team dusting for prints and checking the bank entrance for clues. So far nothing. The guy must have been wearing gloves. We've still got the bank's security video. Maybe we'll get something from that. I'll keep you posted," Zamika added with a dismissive nod in Ryan's direction. To Tiny he said, "Send in this niece and I'll question her."

"Go easy on her, she's still shaken up," Ryan growled.

"We stopped using bamboo shoots under the fingernails a few years back, or hadn't you heard?" the agent mocked him.

Tiny looked from one to the other with a big grin. Ryan knew what he was thinking. As far as he was concerned federal officials were all a pain in the butt.

"Courtney doesn't know anything," Ryan maintained.

"I'll be the judge of that. Send her in and then you can wait outside," Zamika disdainfully instructed Tiny, who did not take kindly to being ordered around.

"Anything else I can do for you?" Tiny inquired mockingly. "Get you a turkey sandwich from the diner across the street maybe?"

From the gleam in Tiny's blue eyes Ryan deduced that the selection of turkey hadn't been a random one, but rather a personal reflection on Zamika's personality.

It sailed right over the agent's head. "I already ate. I don't require your assistance any further, either," he added with a dismissive nod toward Ryan. "You can go."

"I'm staying."

"Suit yourself."

"I usually do," Ryan assured him.

COURTNEY FELT NO FEAR at the prospect of being questioned by an FBI agent. She'd already been given a thorough going-over by the queen of interrogations herself, Francis. "Why did Ryan pose as a customer the first time he came to the bank? How long have the two of you known each other?" A dozen more *whys, wheres* and *whens* had crossed Francis's lips before Tiny came to rescue Courtney.

Tiny, who'd once dated Francis and was the only person to ever call her Franny, gently patted Courtney's shoulder with unspoken commiseration as he escorted her to the conference room.

"Thank you for rescuing me," Courtney whispered.

"Any time."

Once inside the conference room, Courtney registered the fact that Ryan was sprawled in a chair with typical nonchalance before she focused her attention on the other man in the room—a younger and much better dressed man.

"I'm Agent Zamika, Ms. Delaney. I need to ask you a few questions."

Courtney nodded, appreciating the businesslike yet deferential tone of his voice. Quite the opposite from the way Ryan talked to her. The only time Ryan deferred to her wishes was when they'd been making love.

Darn it, how did that happen? How did her thoughts return to the forbidden subject of sex within two seconds of Ryan entering them?

Evoking her internal thought police, she wiped her mind clean as she kept her gaze centered on the FBI agent. She relaxed as she and the agent immediately formed an easy camaraderie.

"Delaney," he noted with a pleasant smile. "That's a good Irish name."

"My father was Irish, my mom grew up in Czechoslovakia."

"Really? My folks are Irish and Eastern European, too, only the reverse of yours. My mom's Irish. Do your parents live here in Oregon?"

"No," she replied. "They passed away when I was ten."

"I'm sorry." His voice reflected sincere sympathy. "You must miss them a lot."

"I do," she said, while thinking to herself, *What a nice guy.*

WHAT A JERK! Ryan rolled his eyes in disgust. So the guy had parents. So what? Ryan had parents, too. You didn't hear him going on and on about them.

And he could have. He had great parents. Unlike Courtney, *they* hadn't thrown a fit when he'd become a deputy marshall. Oh sure, they'd teased him some about being the peacemaker in the family, keeping his siblings Jason, the control freak, and Anastasia, aka It's My Turn in the Bathroom, from each other's throats while growing up. But they'd understood. Courtney hadn't.

Just as she apparently couldn't understand that Zamika was a rigidly dysfunctional bureaucrat on the make. Didn't she see what he was up to? Was she completely blind?

She should be giving the guy the cold shoulder. God knew, she was good at that. Ryan had the frost burns to prove how good.

And why had she taken off her jacket? Her white blouse, while more conservative than what the old Courtney would have worn, still showed off the curves of her breasts more than he liked. Well, he did like it, but he didn't like the way Zamika was eyeing her.

If anyone was going to be eyeing Courtney's cleavage it would be him, not some FBI twit who looked as if he'd been born in a suit. It didn't help matters that Ryan's attire was meant to convey nerdiness rather than power. Ryan had actually had to *learn* how to dress like this. It didn't come naturally!

During his rigorous thirteen-week basic training at Glynco he learned the stuff he needed to protect himself—how to shoot straight, how not to get shot, how to drive fast, how to react in a crisis. Along with the basics of law enforcement training, he'd also been required to take a course in Image Awareness where he'd been taught the talent of manipulating one's wardrobe to the requirements of the job. Ryan had no idea what type of clothing would be appropriate for dealing with Courtney. Nothing he did seemed to be working.

"YOU'RE AWFULLY QUIET," Courtney noted as Ryan ate his dinner in silence later that night. She'd changed out of her suit and heels into a pair of black leggings and an oversize turquoise T-shirt. Her feet were bare but her hair remained in its braid, although she had unpinned it from the bun on top of her head.

"Unlike Chatty Charlie, you mean?" Ryan growled.

She paused to frown at him, a piece of lettuce from her chef's salad poised on her fork. "What are you talking about?"

"Charles Zamika. The FBI guy you were flirting with earlier today. I thought you were supposed to be serious about Fred."

"I am."

"Then why were you flashing the green light at Zamika?"

"I was doing no such thing," she denied. "We were merely making polite conversation."

"Yeah, right," he scoffed. "And the Columbia River is just a tiny little stream."

"Careful, your eyes are turning green."

"It's from having to eat all these peanut-butter-and-jelly sandwiches." He dolefully stared down at the food on his plate.

She refused to feel sorry for him. Because if she gave an inch, she knew she'd be cooking three-course meals. She had to ruthlessly squelch any hint of her desire to pamper him. She had to be tough. Besides, she wouldn't put it past Ryan to feign hunger to gain her sympathy. She, however, was willing to play along with his pretense in order to get in a few jabs of her own. "I can't help it if that's the best your employer can do for you. He's the one who said you'd supply your own food."

"He hates me," Ryan noted glumly.

"You have that effect on some people."

"Very funny."

"Agent Zamika didn't appear to like you much, either," she took great pleasure in informing him.

"The feeling is mutual. Who was that woman in the bank this morning?"

Courtney blinked at his abrupt question. "Excuse me?"

"The old woman in the pink jogging suit. The two of you were talking up a storm."

"We were discussing the stupidity of men."

He grinned, but his gaze was penetrating, digging for the truth. "Why don't I believe that?"

Trying to be helpful, Courtney came up with what she thought was a viable reply. "Because you have a distrustful nature?"

Ryan absently rubbed his chin while frowning in concentration. "She looked familiar to me somehow."

Courtney shifted uncomfortably. Anton's disguise had been so good that even *she* hadn't recognized him, so how could Ryan? He had to be making a stab in the dark here. The secret was not to react.

"I've got some fudge ripple ice cream in the

freezer.'' She deliberately made her voice cheerful and carefree. ''Want some?''

''I want your uncle back in protective custody.''

Now Courtney was the one who was silent. Her first loyalty was to her uncle. If he didn't think he'd be safe in custody, then her hands were tied. She couldn't betray his trust.

Feeling edgy, she fired up her hot-air popcorn maker. Minutes later she grabbed the bowl of hot buttered popcorn and headed for the living room and her VCR.

''I've had enough excitement for one day,'' she stated. ''I need to watch something soothing.'' After sticking a video into the machine, she plunked down on the couch.

''Only you would think that cartoons are soothing.'' He grinned as he sat beside her.

Grabbing a big pillow to sit on, she slithered onto the floor from the couch, not trusting herself to be that close to him. Ryan was unfazed by her departure. Instead he scooted over so that he sat directly behind her, his legs bracketed around her like muscular bookends.

She couldn't count the number of times she'd sat this way when they'd been together. In those days she'd rest her cheek against his knee and curl her arms around his powerful thighs. Not that she'd ever been docile.

The chemistry had always been volatile between them, creating arguments the way hot summer nights created storms. But they'd soon passed, often with

Ryan teasingly telling her that she was entitled to her own opinion...even if it was wrong.

Sometimes she suspected he just liked provoking her because he enjoyed their making up so much. But it was also true that they were two very different personalities. She'd worn her heart on her sleeve in those days, while he'd hidden his emotions beneath an endearing but nonetheless impenetrable layer of humor.

"Relax," he murmured. "You're so uptight you're about ready to crack."

His hands lighted on her shoulders with familiarity. He kept up a steady flow of conversation, but nothing that required her participation. She just had to sit there and enjoy—enjoy the brush of his thumb against her nape, the slide of his fingers against the tight tendons of her neck. He'd always had an incredible talent for finding that one spot that was knotted with tension.

"I'm telling you, I had the worst clothes in that sting operation," Ryan was saying in a low voice laced with amusement. "Even worse than that time I had to dress like a psychedelic golfer. Neon checked pants. Bright purple shirt. But dressing up as the mascot for the Seattle Seahawks was the worst. The good news was the operation worked. We conned a dozen federal felons into showing up at our bogus headquarters to pick up the season tickets they'd supposedly won. Along with a free trip to the Superbowl. Instead they ended up with a free trip back to the penitentiary."

"So what you're telling me is that basically all you marshals do is dress up in funny clothing, huh?"

"You betcha," he cheerfully agreed.

There it was, that way he had of blindsiding her. She'd expected him to take offense, almost wanted him to so that this closeness wouldn't keep tugging her in.

"In that case, I can see why you'd want the job," she said.

"I wanted the job because I like chasing bad guys and keeping the peace. Even as a kid, I was the peacemaker in my family."

"You never told me that before."

"You left before I had the chance."

Was that true? Would he have explained his actions to her had she stayed? "It's not like I left without giving you the opportunity to talk to me."

"We were both pretty angry by then. Could be that we both made a few mistakes."

Having said that, Ryan proceeded to undo her braid and comb his fingers through her long hair. She wanted to believe him, wanted to think that he was willing to acknowledge that he'd been wrong to do what he'd done. But there was so much at stake.

On the TV screen one cartoon ran into the next, Mr. Magoo morphing into the Pink Panther and then the Road Runner, while Ryan simply continued threading his warm fingers through her hair until she was lost in the magic of the good things they had together, not the least of which was this incredible sense of contentment at simply being together. She'd never felt that way before or since. As if he were her home.

But she couldn't trust Ryan's motives, not with him after her uncle. He could just be telling her what she wanted to hear so that she'd be more cooperative in his quest to capture her uncle. No, she couldn't trust him and she couldn't trust herself around him. Not yet.

As if on cue, the videotape ran out. Scrambling to her feet, she winced as one of them tingled from almost falling asleep. "It's getting late." She grabbed her empty popcorn bowl and headed for the kitchen.

Courtney was standing in front of the sink, wiping down the counter, when she heard the loud crash.

7

"WHAT WAS THAT?" Ryan demanded, rushing to the kitchen doorway.

"It wasn't me," Courtney hurriedly assured him. "It sounded like it came from downstairs. Jeez, I've heard Red cooking up a storm downstairs before, but never that loud. I must have jumped a foot just now. It sounded like broken glass."

Instead of answering, Ryan reached for his gun before barking out an order. "Get in the bathroom. *Now.* Lock the door behind you. If I'm not back in five minutes—" he tossed her the cellular phone from his pocket "—call the police."

"Where are you going?"

"Downstairs to check things out. Now get in the bathroom. Come on, get moving." He helped her on her way by hustling her down the hallway. This was the first time she'd seen him with his gun drawn. It should have scared her witless and it did. But there was simply no excuse for the excitement zipping through her entire body.

Okay, so he had his hand on her arm, but even that shouldn't have brought out this breathless thrill. Courtney chalked the reaction up to her wild side, the one she was trying get rid of. That's what was making her fantasize about ravishing Ryan right there and then.

She slammed the door on her thoughts as she slammed the bathroom door. She must still be a little jittery from the attempted robbery earlier in the afternoon. That had to be why she was susceptible to wild fantasies about Ryan.

She prayed that the noise actually was caused by her neighbor. Maybe Red had broken a tray full of glasses. That's what it had sounded like—a lot of glass breaking.

Granted it was a little late to be cooking, after ten, but Red wasn't one to keep to a traditional schedule.

Flipping down the toilet seat lid, Courtney tried to make herself comfortable. Her thoughts kept returning to Ryan's earlier words, before he'd turned all bossy and shoved her into the bathroom. *Could be that we both made a few mistakes.* Had he been sincere? Could she afford to let herself believe in him again? Could she afford not to?

BRUTUS HADN'T volunteered for this job, but after Jimbo had botched up his assignment at the bank, he had no choice but to do this himself. He'd done his legwork ahead of time. He'd double-checked the address to make sure he had the right place, checking it against the printout from the Department of Motor Vehicles records. And he'd waited until the lights in the apartment had gone out, then waited another hour just to be safe.

He'd carefully used a glass cutter, but that had taken forever, so he'd ended up using a crowbar to smash in the window. Just get in, grab the girl and get out. Fast.

The moment he entered the darkened room, he heard a man roar, "Brutus!"

Startled, Brutus turned. "What? Who's there?"

The answer came in the form of action rather than words. He didn't register the growl until too late. By then the vicious dog had leapt onto him, digging its teeth into Brutus's butt.

At first he thought it must be a Doberman, but the thing was smaller, its teeth sharper.

"Get him, Brutus, get him!"

The dog growled in response.

Howling, Brutus leapt back out the bedroom window with the vicious little mutt still attached to his backside.

RYAN HEARD THE howling as he approached the downstairs apartment. When the door was yanked open, he raised his gun...right in Red's direction.

"Man, we've got to stop meeting like this," the startled biker declared.

Swearing under his breath, Ryan lowered his weapon. "What's going on?"

"Some idiot tried to break into my place. There you are." Red's voice changed drastically as he sweetly murmured, "Come to Poppa."

Ryan blinked and took a wary step back, wondering if the guy had gone off the deep end before noticing the little runt of a mutt at their feet.

Red picked up a little fuzzball in his arms. "My

guard dog here got a piece of the robber's hind end. Good job, Brutus. Good dog.''

Guard dog? Ryan had seen steaks that were bigger. "Yeah, well, did you get a look at the guy?"

"You bet. And you know, the strange thing was the guy turned around and said 'What' when I sicced Brutus on him.''

"He turned around when you said 'Brutus'?"

"Yeah. Weird, huh?"

Not so weird. So Brutus Zopo had decided to come after Courtney himself rather than send one of his inept lackeys to do it.

Which meant they knew where she lived. Or close enough. Ryan remembered her telling him that she hadn't changed her driver's license records to reflect her move to the apartment upstairs.

Ryan had to get her someplace safe.

"I THOUGHT YOU were never coming back!" Courtney exclaimed the instant Ryan knocked on the bathroom door and gave her the all clear. "What happened down there? I heard howling. Was it Red?"

"No, it was Brutus."

"Red's dog?" Courtney knew how attached Red was to his pet. "The poor little thing. What was wrong with it?"

"Nothing. But I'm talking about Brutus Zopo. The Zopos have located you. Start packing."

She blinked at him. "Excuse me?"

"You heard me. Start packing."

"Why?"

"Because I plan on taking you someplace safe."

"And where would that be?"

"Why the twenty questions?" he retorted in exasperation. "Can't you just once say, 'Fine, Ryan I'll do whatever you say'?"

"Not in this lifetime," she replied sweetly.

"A man can dream, can't he?" Ryan sighed and got this long-suffering look on his face. "Okay, let's see if I can explain it to you slowly. The bad guys are after you to use you as leverage to get to your uncle. They've tracked you down, and broken into your apartment building in a thwarted attempt to snatch you. I suspect that the botched robbery attempt at the bank this afternoon was another of their plans to kidnap you gone awry. Neither of these two occurrences are a good thing. Are you with me so far?"

She smacked his arm, infuriated by his deliberately condescending tone. "Don't treat me like an idiot."

"Then stop acting like one."

"I am not."

"Are too."

"Am not."

"This is ridiculous." Grabbing her in his arms, Ryan kissed her with a forcefulness that reflected his frustration, his hunger and his fears. Courtney returned his kiss with a passion that reflected her inability to hold back. His arms encircled her, his fingers caressing the small of her back, sliding beneath the waistband of her black leggings to tantalize her with the promise of further intimacies.

When the need for oxygen finally made him lift his mouth from hers, she got the strength to put some distance between them. Glaring at him, she said, "If you think you can kiss me into submission…"

"Yes?"

Her glare dissolved into a grin. "You're right."

"I am?"

"No." She had to laugh at the way his adorable jaw dropped. "I just wanted to throw you for a loop."

"Honey, you've done that since the first moment I met you on that riverboat casino," he drawled.

His rueful look was laced with lingering heat. She could still taste him on her lips. Now she could feel his gaze on her as he slowly explored her body, the path of his eyes over her body leaving a sizzling trail of excitement.

Things were getting too hot, she thought while fanning her flushed cheeks with one hand. Catching the gleam of satisfaction in his lopsided smile, she dropped her hand to wrap her arms around her middle in an attempt to shield her reaction from him. "Will you at least tell me where we're going?"

"No. You'll find out soon enough. Now go pack and be quick about it."

"Do you order all your prisoners around like this?"

"You bet. I also handcuff them."

"Don't even think about it," she warned him. "Get that look right off your face."

Ryan blinked with feigned innocence. "What look?"

"The one where you're imagining me handcuffed, to a bedpost, no doubt." She shot him a wry glance. "You think I can't read you like a book?"

"I think you're stalling," he noted, eyes narrowing. "Why is that? You don't think the danger is real?"

"No, it's not that." She was wondering how she'd let Anton know where she'd be, that's why she was hesitating. How would her uncle find her if Ryan whisked her away without saying a word? She couldn't exactly leave him a note. "What about my job?"

"I'll call Fred and have him give you a few days off."

Her alarm grew. "I can't afford to take that much time off. I don't have any vacation time coming for another eight months."

"You can't afford to stay here. Now stop arguing. Unless you want me to pack for you?"

The idea of him going through her underwear and nightie drawer made her palms go sweaty and her heartbeat go bananas. Jeez, she was acting like a teenager here. She had to get her act together.

Ryan was right, the danger was real. Not only from the Zopo brothers but also from Ryan himself, at least as far as her heart was concerned. She was falling for him all over again. For his lopsided grin, for the simple pleasure of his company, for the way he made her feel so alive, for the way he stubbornly kept after her to be herself, for the way he was trying to protect her and keep her safe from harm.

But his keeping her safe from harm was putting her in danger of having her heart broken again. It was safer to keep her distance. Her head knew that. Now if only her blasted body would cooperate.

"ARE WE LOST?" she demanded three hours later. She was seated beside him in his nondescript sedan, the lights from the instrument panel creating a green glow in the otherwise dark interior. Since they'd left her apartment, Ryan had been quiet and so had she. Until now. "Tell me we're not lost. It feels like we've been going around in circles for ages."

"We have."

"Great." Her voice was glum. "And I suppose you're going to pull that guy stuff and refuse to ask for directions. Am I right?"

"I don't need to ask for directions, because we're not lost," he stated confidently.

"Of course not." Now her inflection was mocking. "You meant for us to be going in circles."

"I certainly did."

"What on earth for?"

"In case anyone was following us."

She craned her head to nervously look out the back window. "You think they are?"

"No. But it's better to be safe than sorry."

"If you liked playing it safe you wouldn't be doing such dangerous work," Courtney retorted. "Most people see trouble, they head in the opposite direction. But you, you run right into it."

"It's my—"

She interrupted him. "Your job. I know. I'm trying to figure out *why* it's your job. What appeal it has for you."

"You could have asked this three years ago."

"You could have told me."

In the faint light caused by a passing car she saw

him nod. Was it his way of acknowledging that he'd made mistakes in their relationship in the past? All he said was, "I'm good at what I do."

"You're good at a lot of things." The words slipped out before she could stop them.

"Oh, yeah?" She could feel the speculative look he shot her way. "Like what?"

"Like driving me crazy. Now talk."

"You first. How exactly do I drive you crazy?"

"Well, hustling me off to an unknown destination is a pretty good start."

"If you must know, we're headed for the coast. It's for your own protection."

"And that's another thing. This attitude you have that you always know best."

"That's because I do," he said calmly.

"Hah!" She shoved a strand of her long hair behind one ear. "I'll have you know I got along just fine for the past three years."

"Just fine if you consider beige to be your favorite color and bland your favorite flavor."

She was infuriated by his words and his attitude. "You're just upset that I've made a good life in Fell without you."

"That's ridiculous. And there's no way that a life with Fred the Friendly Banker in it could be a good one."

"He cares for me more than you do."

"He cares for his bank more than he cares for anything. Did you see the guy panic when the FBI came in? He was practically reeling from the threat to his bank's reputation."

Automatically she leapt to Fred's defense. "Any responsible banker would be upset after an attempted burglary."

"I didn't see him checking up on you."

Courtney had noticed that omission herself and she certainly didn't appreciate Ryan pointing it out to her.

"Instead he seemed protective of his computer and his office, making sure no one touched either one of them. Makes me wonder what the guy is hiding." Ryan's voice sounded reflective.

"You think everyone is hiding something," she scoffed.

"Because they usually are."

"In that case, what are you hiding?"

"You," he immediately answered. "From the bad guys. Remember?"

"How could I forget when I'm having such a good time?" She stared out the windshield at their car's headlights bouncing off the pavement, the yellow dotted lines streaking past them with monotonous regularity. "I have to tell you that I've always longed to go aimlessly driving around in circles all night. It's been a lifetime goal of mine."

"Then I'm glad to have helped you accomplish it." He was unfazed by her sarcasm. "Anything else I can do for you?"

"Yes," she muttered, shifting in her seat. "You can find a rest stop or gas station because I need to use the bathroom."

"I told you to go before we left your place," he grumbled with typical male impatience.

"I did. That was hours ago."

"Great."

"Hey, I'm not real thrilled about it myself. The sanitary conditions in those places is hardly anything to write home about."

"I'll stop at the next town," he said.

She wasn't encouraged by that promise. "Do you even know where the next town is?"

"Of course I do."

To give him credit, Ryan found a gas station within fifteen minutes. Then they were back on the road again, backtracking and retracing their route. Meanwhile Courtney was digging into the cooler she'd brought along from her apartment and stuck in the back seat. Perched on her knees on the front seat, her fanny wiggled as she reached into the far corner to get what she was looking for.

"What are you doing now?" Ryan demanded, a thread of male agitation in his voice.

"Nothing." Settling back in her seat, she refastened her seat belt. Munching on her midnight snack, she added, "You know, you still haven't told me why you decided to become a deputy marshal."

But Ryan had bigger fish to fry. "What are you eating?"

"A ham-and-cheese sandwich."

"You had time to make sandwiches before we left? Why didn't you say so?" He sounded outraged by her omission.

"Because you didn't ask me." She tossed his words back at him. "What did you think I had in that cooler?"

"I don't know. More of that health stuff that you

picked up at the market the other day. Do you have another sandwich in there?''

''Sure do. Bean sprouts and tofu. Want it?''

Even in the dim illumination of the car's dashboard lights she could still see him grimace. ''You shouldn't screw up your face like that,'' she couldn't resist chastising him. ''It might stay that way and then where would you be?''

''You sound like my mother.''

''How are your parents?'' She'd met them several times and had liked them immensely.

''They're doing fine.'' Having said that, Ryan immediately returned to the subject of food. ''Were you kidding or is bean sprouts and tofu really all you've got left in that cooler?''

''Well...'' She drew out the suspense before confessing, ''I do have a roast beef sandwich.''

''Great. I'll have that.''

''How are you going to eat while you drive?''

Ryan could have told her that he'd had lots of practice. But that would waste an opportunity to have her closer to him and he wasn't about to let that happen. For the past ten minutes she'd been taunting him with her wiggling fanny in those form-fitting jeans she'd changed into for traveling. It might be dark in the car, but he wasn't blind. He could feel her movements, could feel his body tightening in response. She was doing it deliberately. He just knew it. So he'd take a page out of her book and taunt her for a change.

That fiery kiss they'd shared at her apartment still sizzled in his veins. He was getting to her. It was only a matter of time, and of proximity. Ryan aimed on making the most of both. "You can feed me."

"I can? How kind of you."

"I thought so," he declared virtuously.

At the first brush of his mouth against her fingers, Courtney knew she was playing with fire. But she couldn't seem to find the energy to care. Enveloped in darkness as they were in the car's interior, a cocoon of intimacy formed between them. The hum of the sedan's engine mingled with the soft sound of a jazz station playing on the radio.

Each time Ryan took a bite of his sandwich, he took a bite out of her self-restraint. It was all too easy to let her fingers linger on his lips. All too easy to brush her shoulder against his as she leaned closer to feed him the next bite.

His refusal to talk about his work and his reasons for choosing it should have been a sore spot for her. It served as a reminder that Ryan hadn't changed in the past three years. He still found it hard to share his inner thoughts.

How could she let herself love him again when he didn't trust her enough to talk about his emotions? Feeling her resolve in danger of melting altogether, she stuffed the remainder of the sandwich in his mouth and scooted back to her own corner of the front seat.

"Whamaya?" he mumbled around a sizable chunk of bread and roast beef.

"You shouldn't talk with your mouth full," she primly informed him.

When Ryan finally swallowed, he said, "And you

shouldn't stuff half a sandwich in my mouth. What did you do that for?''

"For the heck of it. For the same reason you seem to have become a deputy.''

"So we're back to that are we?''

"Forget it.'' Kneeling on the front seat, she reached back into the cooler for a can of root beer, careful to keep her distance from Ryan.

"I'd like to forget it, but you keep harping on it. You didn't ask that FBI agent why he joined the agency.''

"That's because I don't care—'' Courtney stopped the instant she realized what she'd been about to reveal.

"Meaning you do care about me,'' he completed, sounding altogether too darn smug about it.

"Meaning I care about my uncle's safety. And if staying with you a few more days will ensure that...''

Ryan interrupted her. "The only way of ensuring your uncle's safety is for him to turn himself in. It's not too late.''

"You don't give up, do you?'' She took a sip of root beer before adding, "I've heard you're like fly-paper.''

"How would you know that?'' Ryan's voice was quiet.

Too late she remembered that Anton had been the one who had told her. "Someone mentioned it.'' Her reply was offhand, but his persistence was immediate.

"Someone who?''

"I don't remember. Your boss, I suppose.''

"He doesn't know about that nickname. In fact, the

last time someone called me that was when your uncle was with me.''

Courtney tried not to let her panic show. "You're making a mountain out of a molehill here."

"Am I?" His voice remained calm as he added, "So how did your uncle like dressing up as a woman?"

Startled, Courtney choked on her root beer. The carbonated bubbles went up her nose as she coughed and sputtered.

Ryan swore succinctly. "I knew it. I knew that woman at the bank looked familiar."

Courtney lifted her chin a notch or two. "I don't know what you're talking about."

"Cut the act. I know that was your uncle at the bank."

"You've got a vivid imagination."

"I should have realized it earlier," Ryan muttered to himself. "With his dramatic training, Anton would be great at disguising his appearance. I just hadn't expected him to go to such extremes. I should have. I mean this is the maniac who climbed out of a window no sane person would have attempted."

"My uncle is not a maniac!"

"And then there's you." Ryan shot her a look that made her shiver in her seat. "Trying to seduce me to distract me from my work."

"What?" Her voice could have scalded the paint right off the car's exterior. "Listen, buddy, if there's any seducing going on, you're the one who's been doing it. You're the one who's kissing me every two minutes."

"You wish."

She saw red. "I wish you hadn't barged back into my life. I wish you'd left me alone!" she shouted at him.

"I didn't ask for this job, I can tell you that," he shouted back at her. "I tried to get out of it."

She'd suspected as much, but his words still were like a slap in the face.

"Damn, that didn't come out right," Ryan muttered.

Clamping her teeth down on her bottom lip to prevent more angry comments from tumbling forth, Courtney refused to say another word for the remainder of the trip. Clouds scuttled across the moon, further limiting visibility.

Another hour went by. She could tell that much because of the digital readout on the dashboard. The jazz program on public radio had been replaced with classical music as Dvořák's symphony *From the New World* filled the silence.

The last time Courtney had heard this music, she'd made dinner for Anton and they'd spent the evening reminiscing. She prayed he was safe.

When Ryan finally pulled the car to a stop, the uncharacteristic hesitancy of his voice immediately captured her attention. "We're here. But before we go in...uh...I guess there's something I should... warn you about the place."

8

COURTNEY SQUINTED through the windshield in the pale moonlight, trying to make out the shape of the building just up the driveway. "Warn me about what? Where are we?" Rolling down the passenger window, she could hear the crashing surf of the ocean and smell the salty air.

"We're on the coast," Ryan replied shifting in his seat. "A ways outside of Newport. The house belongs to a buddy of mine."

"Does it have indoor plumbing?" she asked suspiciously, trying to pinpoint the reason for Ryan's discomfort.

"Yes. It's just that he has sort of strange decorating tastes."

"So what? I'm hardly Martha Stewart," she retorted. "Besides, I don't aim on being here very long."

"It shouldn't take the authorities long to track down Brutus Zopo," Ryan told her. "His brother is implicated as well—he appears to have been driving the getaway car. I checked that out while you were packing. We have another witness who described the car, and your neighbor can identify Brutus. I figure it's a matter of hours, twenty-four maybe, forty-eight tops.''

"Seems a long way to come for twenty-four hours," she murmured getting out of the car with eagerness. She was sick and tired of driving around in circles.

Holding the car door open for her, Ryan lifted one eyebrow. "You want to stay here longer?"

"That's not what I meant."

"I didn't think so." As he inclined his head toward the house, his brown hair fell over his forehead. It was all she could do not to reach out and brush the rebellious strands back into place. "So, are you ready to face Dean's Lair?" he added.

"That's really what he calls this place?" She laughed nervously, joining him on the front porch. Constructed out of weathered wood that had turned silvery in the salty air, the place seemed to sprawl out in various levels and directions. "What is it, a bachelor pad from the seventies? James Bond meets Steve Martin?"

"Something like that. He hides the key here...."

She squinted and then blinked. "That's a statue—"

"Of a woman's breast. Yes, I know. It's also the doorbell, but if you press the side just right..."

She watched his fingers skimming over the pale marble surface and was struck with the memory of his hands on her own bare skin. His fingers were a reflection of the man, rugged and powerful, nothing delicate or dainty about him.

"Aha." A hidden compartment popped out of the

smooth marble, disturbing its perfect symmetry. Inside was the key.

"That's impressive," she had to admit.

"You should see the andirons in the fireplace. Done by the same artist."

It was the first thing she saw when she entered the house. Moonlight shot through the skylight, lighting their way to the huge natural stone fireplace against the entire left wall. Not only were the andirons a pair of women's legs, they were life-size versions, their pointed toes aimed toward the carved wooden mantel. Above the mantel was a huge fishnet complete with a colorful wooden mermaid figurehead, like those that used to grace the bow of a large ship.

"So far I'd say this place is more Pablo Picasso than Steve Martin," she proclaimed wryly.

"You haven't seen the bedroom yet."

There was only one, and that was enough. Everything was done in leopard print. The bedspread, the draperies, even the carpeting. Three walls and the ceiling were mirrored, while a black marble fireplace with a pair of leopard andirons took up the far wall.

"Cool," she murmured, peering out the windows.

"You really think so?"

"Sure." She opened the heavy curtains to show the breathtaking ocean view. White-crested waves broke onto a seemingly endless expanse of beach, all bathed in moonlight, which was reflected back in the mirrored walls. "Pretty incredible, huh?"

Ryan nodded, but it wasn't the view he was admiring, it was her. After packing at the apartment, she'd changed into jeans and a white T-shirt. The denim lovingly clung to her bottom. Because the night was cool, she'd tossed on a black leather jacket that was too big for her and looked like it might have been a hand-me-down from Red. The end result was a bad-girl look that made his blood run hot.

Her hair was loose and wavy as it cascaded over the leather like a waterfall of gold silk. He remembered threading his fingers through it earlier that night, when she'd sat on the floor at his feet. Touching her then had been part heaven part hell. He'd wanted to do more than just give her a neck rub. He'd wanted to tumble her onto the carpet and make her his. The way she had been before. When they'd been together. Cleaved to him, naked flesh to naked flesh.

Because no other woman had ever made him feel complete the way she did. He could only hope that once this mess with her uncle was straightened out maybe they could start over again. If she trusted him again. If she didn't hold a grudge against him for bringing in her uncle. Pretty big ifs. Things would be so much easier if she'd just cooperate.

But then nothing about Courtney had ever been easy.

"Take a look at this." Her excited voice broke into his thoughts. He tracked her into the bathroom opening off the master bedroom.

"Wow!" When Ryan joined her, she made no effort to hide her awe. The bathroom was bigger than her present living room and bedroom combined. A mural was painted on the walls, depicting life in ancient Rome.

Well, now that she looked closer she realized it

wasn't exactly a depiction of everyday life. It was an orgy. She blinked at the entwined couple in the corner before noting, ''I'm not sure that's anatomically possible.''

Ryan's muffled chuckle made her spin around. Was he laughing at her? ''What?''

''It's just that you sound like your old self.''

His warm words stole into her heart. She had to stay tough. So she used humor to keep her distance. ''How kind of you to call me old.''

''That's not what I meant.''

She knew what he meant and it made her edgy to talk about it. Staying in these hedonistic surroundings made her attraction to Ryan even more powerful. On her own turf, in her own apartment, she'd been able to withstand his attempts to romance her. Would she be able to continue the fight here?

She focused on her surroundings to distract herself from Ryan's presence. ''I love this bathroom. Not so much the artwork as the tub. I want to live in that tub. It's the size of my kitchen.'' The sunken marble tub was pink-veined, like the marble columns flanking it. She made a shooing motion with both hands. ''Get out of here, I'm taking a bath.''

''Now?'' He gave her a startled look. ''It's four in the morning.''

''I don't care. Now move.''

He didn't budge. ''What if you fall asleep and drown?''

Putting her hands on her hips, she stared at him in exasperation. ''When did you start to be such a worrywart? Unless this is your charming way of suggesting that you stay to monitor my safety during my bath?'' She arched a brow at him.

He gave her a lopsided grin. ''Now that you mention it...''

''Forget about it. You can sit outside the door if you want.''

''You know what I want.''

''Yes, I do.'' She took his arm and led him out the door. But before she closed it, she added, ''You want to capture my uncle.''

''YOU GOT THE TWO of them alone together in a romantic seaside getaway. Well done, Muriel!'' Betty slapped a high five on Muriel's open palm as the two of them danced across the black marble mantelpiece of the bedroom fireplace. Betty had to hold up the hem of the baggy Columbo-type raincoat with one hand or risk tripping over it as she kicked up her heels. ''Way to go, girl!''

''There is indeed a way to go,'' Hattie chastised, demurely sitting on the corner of the mantel while delicately shaking sand out of one of her silk slippers dyed the same apricot as her dress. ''Quite a long way.''

''She's still in a snit from landing on the beach instead of the bedroom her first try,'' Muriel told Betty.

''Oh, horsefeathers,'' Hattie retorted, standing up to glare at both her sisters. ''I am not in a snit. I'm just saying that I still see no sign that these two are ready to admit they're made for each other.''

''What about that talk they had in the car getting

here?'' Muriel demanded, running her hands through her short hair and thereby making her cowlick stick up. ''There was plenty of soul baring going on.''

''That was just the beginning.'' Looking at her sister's wild hair, Hattie hastily patted her own silvery curls to make sure they were perfectly coiffed. ''And then they ended up fighting and not speaking to each other the rest of the trip. As for that scene in the bathroom we just witnessed, it was all sizzle and no fire. Courtney ended things by referring to her uncle. She hasn't forgotten or forgiven.''

Muriel glared at Hattie. ''You're just worried that you're going to have to deal with Anastasia sooner than you thought you would and that my speedy success with Ryan will put you to shame.''

''You wish!'' Hattie stamped her dainty foot. ''I never heard of anything so ridiculous in all my life.''

''I don't know,'' Betty mused with a wide grin. ''That color fight you and Muriel had was right up there on the ridiculous scale.''

Hattie lifted her chin with aristocratic hauteur. ''Scoff all you want, but I'm telling you, I don't think things are settled between Ryan and Courtney yet by any means.''

''I BLAME MYSELF for this. I should never have trusted you to do such an important job yourself.'' Caesar patted Brutus's cheek so hard it stung.

''I didn't do it all myself,'' Brutus blurted out, aware of the danger inherent in his older brother's soft voice.

''Ah, yes. The disaster with that half-witted brother

of the woman you are seeing. Yes, that was a brilliant thing to do. That alone should have warned me that you were not up to handling this job. But no, I believed you when you said you could take care of matters. And what happens? You end up with dog bites on your butt. A Zopo, once the proudest of all families, now has to live down the fact that you were bested by a dog.'' Caesar shook his head with intense sorrow.

''But it was a huge dog, Caesar, the biggest dog you ever saw. Must have been part bear.''

''I did see the dog and the only relation it had was to a teddy bear. It was a little ball of fluff.''

''With huge teeth,'' Brutus interjected. ''I had to have a dozen stitches.''

''And now, thanks to your big mouth, the authorities are after us. Because you not only broke into the wrong apartment, you answered to the name of Brutus and then had the stupidity to let the idiot in that apartment see your face.''

Brutus hung his head in shame. ''I wasn't thinking.''

''That much is obvious.'' Caesar rubbed his hand against his jaw. ''What is not so clear is how we are to proceed from here.''

''I will do whatever you tell me.''

''You will do nothing!'' Caesar's soft voice took on a dangerous edge. ''From now on, I am in charge. And I will make sure that things are done properly. You can be assured of that.''

COURTNEY SLEPT LATE the next morning, waking to the sound of her stomach growling. A groggy glance

at her watch told her it was nearly one in the afternoon.

By the time she padded into the kitchen, fresh from
another bath and dressed in jeans and a red T-shirt,
she was starving. Ryan was on the kitchen extension,
laughing into the phone.

The sound slid down her spine like a lover's touch.
It wasn't fair. He was still wearing the same basic
outfit he'd worn when he'd walked back into her
life—jeans, a T-shirt which was khaki green today,
and a flannel shirt. The problem was that his jeans
molded his body to perfection, the T-shirt—which
stretched magnificently across his muscular chest—
brought out the green in his eyes and the green-and-
black flannel covered his broad shoulders with soft
seductiveness.

Curses. She needed caffeine in her system before
she could be expected to fight her love for Ryan. Not
love, she hurriedly corrected herself. Attraction. Physical attraction.

She poured herself a huge mug of coffee and drank
it black before even noticing the entwined couples
painted on the side of the mug. She almost dropped
it on the floor when she realized what it was depicting.

"Your friend has a definite problem," Courtney
told Ryan the moment he was off the phone.

"And good morning to you, too."

"I'm serious. I was okay with the statue out front,
with the leggy andirons and even the mural in the
bathroom. But this is too much. Where's my cooler?"

Spying it in the corner, she opened it and dug through the melting ice before lifting out her Yogi Bear mug, filled with fresh cherries. "That's better." Dumping the fruit out on a plate, she rinsed her mug before filling it with coffee.

"Dean may seem strange if you judge him from this place, but he's okay," Ryan replied. "He was my partner for a while, before he got transferred. He's from a wealthy family and likes shocking people."

"He's doing a pretty good job of it," she murmured, blowing on the hot coffee and taking another cautious sip.

"He's okay. I should know. Being a good judge of character is a necessity in my line of work."

"A good judge of character, huh?" She shot him a mocking look. "Is that why you mistook Red for a dangerous character?"

A flush of embarrassment stole into Ryan's cheeks as he growled, "When I'm around you, my internal radar gets messed up."

"Oh, that's great to hear," she retorted, setting her mug on the counter before turning to face him. "I'm being protected by a guy with a messed up instincts."

"I'll tell you one thing that isn't messed up." Tugging her into his arms with one smooth move, he kissed her. It was fast and it was intense. He tasted like coffee and temptation as his arms enfolded her, urging her lower body into the cradle of his denim-clad hips. She fit him perfectly, her body conforming to his. She was moist softness where he was throbbing hardness.

Pleasure filled every particle of her body. She loved

the rub of his thighs as she parted her legs and melted against him. She murmured her excitement as he shifted his hand, the one that had been lying in wait on her rib cage, until it covered her breast. Her thin T-shirt and bra provided no protection against the forbidden enchantment of his touch.

Reeling drunkenly in a world awash with physical elation, she touched him as she'd longed to. His rebellious hair was still as thick and surprisingly silky as she remembered. She slid her other hand beneath his flannel shirt, which was as soft as she'd thought it would be. Just as he was as solid and powerful as she knew he would be. She slowly trailed her fingers up the ridges of his spine beneath his T-shirt.

When his caresses to her breast became more intimate, she grabbed handfuls of the cotton material of his T-shirt as she was buffeted with erotic delight. Being with him this way felt so incredibly good. And all the while, his mouth consumed hers with electrifying need.

But unlike their previous kisses, this one eventually softened into tenderness. Courtney found that even scarier than his hunger. Because she could fight passion, but not this heartrending gentleness that recalled their first days together when he'd wooed her, seduced her, loved her.

She had to remind herself of the reality. Ryan was only kissing her because he wanted to seduce her into betraying Anton. He'd do anything to catch his man, to protect his career. She couldn't give in. She *couldn't.*

Yanking herself out of his arms, she took two huge

steps away from him, her trembling fingers brushing her lips which still hungered for the touch of his.

"My future is with Fred." She was dismayed with the way her voice wavered thinly.

Ryan shoved a hand through the hair she'd messed up with her caressing fingers. There was a turbulent light in his hazel eyes that didn't bode well for her.

"Interesting thing about Fred," Ryan drawled. "When the FBI did a routine check to make sure the robbery hadn't been an inside job, what did they find? That geeky Fred has been skimming bank funds and embezzling money into his own private accounts."

"What are you talking about?" Her manner was cautious, her voice suspicious.

"I'm talking about embezzlement." He pronounced each syllable slowly and succinctly. "Ninety thousand dollars worth."

"You're making this up," Courtney accused him. "You've never liked Fred and now you're trying to discredit him."

Ryan shrugged off her accusation. "Call the sheriff and ask him. I heard it from Tiny himself, who also told me he's dating Francis again. Talkative fellow, that Tiny. Can you believe he calls her Franny?"

Courtney sank onto a nearby kitchen chair, experiencing the numbness that comes with incredulity. "I don't believe any of this."

"Like I said, you're welcome to call Tiny and check it out with him." His voice turned reflective as he noted, "Now that I think about it, Fred got all flushed and bothered when I pitched him the idea of my being a bank inspector. And then there was his strange behavior after the attempted robbery, the way he tried to keep everyone out of his office.''

Ryan was secretly relieved that the no-good twit was out of the picture. The little weasel hadn't been good enough for Courtney. Ryan had known it from the very start. But Courtney had kept claiming that Fred was the man for her. Not true. Ryan had been the man for her in the past, and he wanted to be again. He just wasn't sure what to do. Everything he seemed to say was wrong.

Courtney was shaking her head and saying, ''But I've only been gone one day.''

''And your job will still be waiting for you when you get back. If you still want it.''

She picked up on that immediately. ''Why wouldn't I want it? I've got rent and utilities to pay, not to mention other expenses.''

He shrugged. ''You can do better, but it's your life.''

''That's right. It is. You'd do well to remember that.''

''And you'd do well to remember that your uncle's life is in danger. That was a stupid stunt he pulled, walking into the bank yesterday dressed as a woman.''

Courtney neither denied nor confirmed Ryan's caustic observation.

The chilliness between them remained throughout that day and forced her to go to bed early. There was no reading material that wasn't X-rated. Thank heavens for public television, where she watched an old classic, *How to Marry a Millionaire,* before finding a cartoon festival on a cable station. But even the antics of Yogi Bear and Scooby-Doo couldn't lift her spirits.

Her prim buttercup yellow cotton pajamas were at odds with her leopard print surroundings as she threw herself on the bed to stare at her reflection in the mirrored ceiling and brood. Her cheerful Bugs Bunny fuzzy slippers were at odds with her dark thoughts. How could she have been so wrong about Fred? She felt as if someone had yanked a rug out from under her. Was there just a tad of relief mixed in with the disbelief? Relief that she wouldn't be tied to Fred and his finicky ways for the rest of her life?

So much for her attempts to have a quiet, well-behaved life.

Sticking out her tongue at her reflection, she rolled onto her stomach, propping her chin on her clasped hands. No, she wasn't stuck with Fred. Her plans for a new respectable and proper life had gone up in smoke. Instead here she was—stuck in Dean's Lair with Ryan, the man she'd once given her heart to. And he had broken it.

No matter how much she tried telling herself she was a different woman now, a much wiser woman, she couldn't help the sinking feeling that history was about to repeat itself.

BRIGHT AND EARLY the next morning, Ryan checked in with Wes Freeze, who took great pleasure in Ryan's bad mood.

"Still wish I'd shot you instead of giving you this assignment?" Wes asked.

Considering the fact that Ryan had gotten little

sleep last night, he wasn't exactly amused by his boss's gloating. "Have the Zopos been arrested for attempted robbery yet?"

"They've disappeared."

"I don't believe this." Ryan shoved an impatient hand through his hair. "Brutus Zopo isn't exactly the sharpest knife in the drawer. How hard can it be to catch up with him?"

"Any leads on Anton Leva yet?"

"He hasn't left the state."

"How do you know that?" Wes demanded.

"Because he came into the bank yesterday."

"And you didn't grab him then?" Wes's voice rose to a roar.

"He was dressed as an old woman in a pink jogging outfit. I didn't realize it was him until much later."

"What about the niece? No luck convincing her to cooperate?"

"I'm working on it."

"Well, get a move on it." Wes's impatience was clear. "We do have other cases, you know. I need you back here. Work is piling up."

After hanging up with Wes, Ryan called in to check his office voice mail. There was a message from his brother, Jason, asking Ryan to call him back about something important.

"You're hard to get ahold of," Jason complained once Ryan got him on the line.

"Hey, you weren't too happy to talk to me last time," Ryan retorted.

"Let me see…. Was that right after you sent me a

load of manure at work, or was it the time you kept pouring gasoline in my new car so that I thought it was getting seventy miles to the gallon.''

Ryan grinned as he fondly recalled, "That was one of my better practical jokes."

"I'm glad you thought so," Jason grumbled, "because I sure didn't."

"No imagination, that's your problem, big brother." Ryan's voice was mocking. Jason was the eldest only by a few minutes, but he never let his two siblings forget that fact. Ryan could imagine his brother back in Chicago, his desk neat despite the piles of paperwork he had to complete in his job as a prosecutor in the U.S. Attorney's office. Jason loved order in his life. "So what's up? Your message said it was important."

"I'll say it is. I'm getting married."

"Really?" The news wasn't that big a surprise to Ryan, who knew Jason's propensity to plan out his life. Now that they were both thirty-three, he figured his brother had probably earmarked this as the year for marriage. Jason was like that. Ryan wasn't. "Let me guess. She's some pristine trophy wife that will look good on the arm of Chicago's most successful prosecuting attorney."

"Wrong. She's Heather Grayson, radio talk show hostess of 'Love on the Rocks.'"

Ryan laughed. "Now who's the practical joker?"

"It's no joke." Even over the phone line, his displeasure was evident.

"Come on," Ryan scoffed. "A friend sent me a tape of her show and it's hilarious. There's no way a woman with that great a sense of humor would put up with a stick-in-the-mud like you, even if you were named Chicago's sexiest bachelor.''

"So does that mean you don't want to be my best man?" Jason's voice was dry.

"You're serious?"

"Damn right, I am," Jason growled but Ryan heard the smile.

"When's the wedding?" he asked.

"August 15."

His brother's reply took him by surprise. It was already mid-June. "That soon?" He shook his head in disbelief before noting, "None of this is like you, Jason."

"So Anastasia takes great pleasure in telling me almost daily."

"And how does our darling sister get along with Heather?" Ryan asked. "Does she like her?"

"Yes, not that I give a damn."

"Liar," Ryan scoffed, knowing that despite their outward antipathy, his two siblings were close. "Well then, provided I can get the time off, I'll be there."

"I'm counting on it. And Ryan, leave your practical joke book in Oregon, understand?"

Ryan was still smiling when he hung up.

"What was that all about?" Courtney asked. She'd walked into the kitchen during the tail end of the conversation and heard enough to know Ryan was speaking to his brother.

"It appears that Jason is getting married."

"You sound stunned by the concept," Courtney noted, sipping her coffee from her Yogi Bear mug.

"I am," he admitted.

"It figures." Tucking her pink oxford shirt more securely into the waistband of her jeans, she then perched on a breakfast nook stool and nibbled on a blueberry granola bar.

"What figures?" Ryan demanded in irritation.

"It figures that something like marriage and commitment would never cross the mind of a man like you."

"And how would you define a man like me?"

"Someone who's afraid of commitment," she said bluntly.

His hazel eyes flashed. "I'm not afraid of anything."

"Of bullets or felons, no," she agreed. "But you are afraid of commitment. Of the responsibility of being in a relationship, of having to think about someone other than yourself."

"Are you accusing me of being selfish?"

She refused to answer his question. She didn't want to fight with Ryan today. So she changed the subject. "What have you heard about Brutus? Have they caught him yet?"

"No. The Zopo brothers are proving to be damned elusive."

"Surprise, surprise," she muttered under her breath.

He heard her and was not amused. "What's that supposed to mean?"

"It means that I'm going crazy being cooped up in here all day!" she replied irritably. "You said it would only be for twenty-four hours. We've already been here longer than that and there's still no sign of them catching the Zopos. I need to get some fresh air. Can't we go out on the beach? It's a gorgeous day outside.'' She pointed to the blue sky visible through the corner window over the kitchen sink.

Ryan shrugged. ''So sit on the deck.''

''I already spent five hours sitting on the deck yesterday. It's not the same. I want out! This is the first sunny day we've had in two weeks. I need to get out in it, take a walk, move around. I could put on a disguise.'' She warmed up to the idea, knowing if she stayed in this love lair another hour with Ryan she'd go crazy. ''There are some women's clothes in the closet. Stay right there. I'll show you what I mean.''

Since Ryan had been deliberately tempting her for days, she couldn't resist turning the tables on him by putting on a leopard print bikini along with a short curly black wig. She hadn't worn anything this daring or revealing in some time and while she'd filled out some, she didn't look half-bad.

Ryan apparently thought so, too, because he went slack-jawed and his hazel eyes glazed over. But beneath that dazed expression was a flare of hungry heat. He went on to practically devour her in a visual caress that went from the top of her head down to her bare toes, leisurely perusing every inch in between.

''You must be kidding.'' His voice sounded raspy and dry, as if he hadn't used it this decade. ''You're not seriously thinking of going out in public dressed or should I say undressed like that?''

''I thought you wanted the old Courtney back,''

she challenged him. "The one who dressed to please herself."

"I'm beginning to see the advantages of the more demure Courtney. There's no way I'm letting you out in that."

She did a pirouette for him. "You don't like it?"

"I like it just fine, but I wouldn't be the only one seeing it. You'd garner too much attention."

His reference to their reason for being there dampened her high spirits somewhat.

"Wasn't there something in the closet more concealing?" he demanded gruffly.

Her next selection was all khaki and made her look as if she were ready to go on safari. There was even a pith helmet on the top shelf.

To give him credit, Ryan got the joke and laughed. Thankfully he didn't insist she wear that getup. "I've seen you in enough khaki. Here, let a pro handle this," he said.

She already knew he was a pro at handling her, from giving her a neck massage to stealing a kiss.

From the closet he selected a pair of jeans two sizes too big for her and a denim shirt with sleeves so long they had to be rolled up several times over. To finish the picture, he grabbed a baseball cap and carefully gathering her hair and wrapping it around his hand, he gently stuffed it beneath the cap. "There." Taking a step back, he looked her over. He added a large pair of garish sunglasses to her ensemble before nodding his approval. "Now from a distance you can't tell if you're male or female. Much better disguise. Until you walk.'' He frowned at her. "Don't sway like that.''

"Like what?''

"That.'' He pointed to her hips.

"I'm more concerned with keeping these loose pants up,'' she muttered, tugging on the belt loops.

"That belt should keep them in place just fine.''

"*Should* being the operative word here. And now you want me to worry about my walk?'' she said in exasperation, shoving the slipping sunglasses back up her nose.

"Just don't make it so girly.''

"How about this?'' She strode across the room with a bowlegged smugness that would have done a cowboy proud.

Ryan cracked up. "You don't approve?'' she demanded, hands on her hips.

"Fine. That will do. So what if people think you've got rocks in your pants. Now here are the rules. You stick close to me, and we don't interact with anyone else.''

"Sure. Fine,'' she hurriedly agreed. "Just get me out of here.''

A few more minutes in his presence and she'd run into his arms and beg him to make love to her. Instead, she was the first one out the door. Or she would have been, had Ryan not grabbed her by the arm and checked things out first before giving her the nod.

She was glad to see he wasn't wearing the green-and-black flannel shirt he'd worn yesterday when she'd melted in his arms. Instead his shirt was shades of brown, drawing attention to his rough-and-tumble hair which was already falling over his high forehead.

Drat, she was doing it again. Drooling over him. Some fresh air should clear her mind.

Following Ryan, she noticed the lazy surefootedness of his walk, not to mention the sexy curve of his denim-covered butt. Curses, she was at it again. Determinedly she switched her attention to her surroundings.

The house had a private staircase leading down to the beach. Courtney hadn't seen it before, because the entrance gate was almost obscured by greenery. The wooden steps were steep and there were plenty of them. She didn't care. It was glorious to be outside. The sun shone down on her, the sea breeze teased her cheeks as seagulls soared up above.

For the rest of the day, she and Ryan roamed the beach, hand in hand, exploring wave-washed coves, listening to the surf and watching the antics of the seagulls.

In one particularly broad expanse of sand, Courtney decided to build herself a sand castle, complete with romantic turrets, using an abandoned child's bucket they'd found.

"Hey, you're pretty good at that," Ryan congratulated her. "Ever thought of entering the Sand Castle Contest they have at Cannon Beach each year?"

"I don't like the competitiveness of contests," she said, rubbing the sand from her nose while wondering how it got there in the first place. "I just like building things for my own enjoyment."

Ryan had gotten plenty of enjoyment from watching her cavorting around the beach earlier. She was like a kid, yet he was very much aware of the woman's body beneath the disguising clothing. Her smile flashed as bright as sunlight on the waves.

She was biting her bottom lip, her expression one of intense concentration as she carefully delineated the castle windows with a stick. She'd already collected a pocketful of sea offerings, from shells to bits of driftwood. These she used to decorate her creation.

"There! I now declare this castle open. Tours start on the hour," she said in her best guide voice.

Ryan imagined the pleasure of touring her body on the hour, of exploring every nook and cranny, of running his hands over every delicious inch of creamy skin.

The sound of children laughing distracted him from his X-rated fantasies. The kids were playing tag with the waves and before he knew it, Courtney had bopped off to join them, her feet bare, the hems of her oversize jeans rolled up to display her dainty ankles.

Swearing under his breath, he quickly checked out the surrounding area, noting that the kids' parents were farther up, keeping a watchful eye. Their calls drew the kids back in their direction, but Courtney continued her game, shrieking as the cold water washed over her feet.

The wind had kicked up and the waves weren't wimpy. They often caught her unawares, splashing up her legs.

Laughing and wet she returned to collapse in the

sand beside him. "Those waves are something else again. They didn't look that big."

"You look about ten."

She arched a brow at him. "On a scale of one to ten you mean?"

"I meant age-wise."

"Gee, thanks."

Courtney felt worlds better after spending the afternoon outdoors. She'd never been one to stay holed up inside for very long.

By the time they finally returned to their temporary home, her feet and calves ached from walking on the sand. A hot bath in the decadent tub helped but not enough. Ryan caught her wincing after dinner.

A few moments later she found herself spread out on her bed, wearing little more than a white cotton robe and a smile.

"Oh, oh, oh," she moaned, "that's so good. Don't stop, don't stop."

"If I'd known giving you a foot massage would get this kind of response, I'd have done it a lot sooner," Ryan said.

He poured more peppermint lotion onto his large hands and started on her left foot. As before he began with the heel, rubbing the ball of his thumb from side to side while working his way toward the sensitive arch. Her skin tingled with grateful appreciation.

Now he was running his bent knuckles over the entire sole. She was going to melt right there on the bed.

Then came the pièce de résistance. Her toes. One

by one he caressed them, massaged them, his hands slick from the lotion.

Once again, her gasps and breathless exclamations of pleasure filled the air. He moved from her feet up her calves, his fingers lingering at the back of her knee.

Courtney wanted him so badly she couldn't see straight. Could you go blind from sexual frustration? She wasn't about to find out, because this was it. The time had come.

9

MAKE LOVE TO ME. She wanted to tell him the words, but they were locked in her throat. Held there by fear and longing.

Then words weren't necessary as Ryan stopped massaging and began caressing. He began with tempting swirls to the backs of her thighs, sliding his fingers beneath the short hem of her robe. Then he smoothed the material against her skin, traveling on top of it, the heat of his touch burning through the white cotton.

Tracing her spine with gentle fingers he tunneled beneath her long golden hair to settle on the back of her neck, brushing the downy hair there, before swirling onward to the curve of her ear. She melted even more. Leaning down, he whispered in her ear. "Tell me what you want."

"You," she whispered in return, rolling onto her back as he straddled her body. The movement created a friction of his hard body rubbing against hers, increasing the aching hunger tenfold.

Pulling his head down to hers, she kissed him. The hunger was immediate, the passion familiar. This was Ryan. The man she loved. The man she'd always loved. She didn't want to think, she just wanted to feel—feel his arms around her, his hands slipping beneath her thin robe to caress her.

At first he was barely touching her, his fingers grazing but not lingering over the curves of her breasts. Her nipples tingled with the need to know the feel of his touch. And then he cupped her in the palm of his large hand as the robe slid away, leaving nothing between her creamy skin and his long fingers.

Their kiss took on a new level of intimacy. So did his caresses. He stroked the underside of one breast with his index finger, teased the rosy crest with the ball of his thumb until it firmed in lush arousal. Then his seductive mouth descended as he tempted her nipple with his tongue.

She gripped his shoulders, pleasure swirling through her. "I want you," she gasped. "Now."

"Shhh," he soothed her, gently combing his fingers through her hair, lifting it away from her face and spreading it across the black silk sheets as if it were her crowning glory. And all the while, he was kissing her parted lips, his thumb rubbing the skin beneath her ear in a mesmerizing motion that spoke of building passion. Because his other hand was also rubbing, farther down, in the one spot that yearned for his touch.

In Dvořák's *New World* symphony there was a passage that had been made into a song called "Going Home" and that's what it felt like when she was wrapped in Ryan's arms. As if she'd come home. As if this was where she was meant to be.

She loved him. The knowledge slipped into her heart. She'd never really stopped loving him. That's why she hadn't been able to get this intimate with another man. Because it had never felt this right.

Their lovemaking took on a dreamlike quality, an erotic celebration created not just by the cool slipperiness of the black silk sheets and the surrounding mirrors but by the enduring passion that flared between them. The bed was king-size and they made use of every inch of it as Ryan tossed off his clothing with hasty urgency. When he was as naked as she was, he grabbed a latex condom from his jeans pocket. Once protection was taken care of he rejoined her, his lips consuming hers with unmistakable hunger, the thrust of his tongue imitating the thrust of his body as he joined with her.

Courtney lovingly welcomed him. The ecstasy went beyond sensation, transporting her into a new realm of wonder and bliss. Bending her knees, she rolled over him to perch atop his glorious body and smile down at him with Eve-like triumph.

"You like that?" His voice was raspy with passion.

"Mmm." Her breathy sigh was catlike. "Don't you?"

"Yes," he growled before showing her exactly how much.

Completion came quickly as her entire being hovered on the peak of excitation before beginning the free fall into total satisfaction.

THE NEXT MORNING, Courtney woke to see a reflection of herself in the mirrored ceiling. She was smiling. And she looked as well loved as one of those naked nymphs in the mural on the bathroom wall.

Her gaze sought out Ryan, before registering the sound of the shower running. So he'd been unable to resist trying out the deluxe shower in her bathroom. She wished he'd wakened her to join him. Some of her muscles gave a twinge as she stretched. Remembering what they'd done in the middle of the night and again just before dawn made her blush.

The sound of the phone ringing startled her. She wondered whether or not she should answer it before recalling that Ryan had arranged to have her calls forwarded to this number.

"Hello?" Her greeting was hesitant, her voice still husky with sleep and remembered passion.

"Good morning, *malenka*," Anton declared cheerfully. "I didn't wake you, did I?"

Pulling the sheet around her, Courtney sat up in bed while casting a wary look toward the bathroom where Ryan was still taking his shower. "I'm so glad to hear from you," she whispered into the receiver. "I've been so worried."

"And I about you. You sound…different."

"Must be because of call forwarding."

"Are you sure it is not Ryan? Having your old boyfriend staying with you, alone, this is not a good thing. You have done nothing to regret?"

Courtney felt uncomfortable discussing her intimate relationship with Ryan. "Let's talk about you. Are you okay?"

"I am fine. But I have had to move. I can tell you now. Before I was hiding out in Fred's basement. I remember you telling me he never went down there.

And he keeps so much food in his freezer he never noticed that some of it was missing.''

"Fred's basement!" She couldn't believe it. Her uncle had been only a few blocks away.

"I had to move because the police were there when I returned from taking a walk. No one recognized me in my disguise as an old woman, but such a close call made me nervous. They took Fred away.''

"He's been charged with embezzling money from the bank," Courtney said, keeping her voice low.

"Ah, I thought perhaps they were after me. Well, as you know, I was no fan of Fred's''

"No, I didn't know that." This came as news to her. "You never told me.''

"Do not get me wrong. I appreciate the use of his basement, even if it was without his knowledge.''

"What are your plans now?" she asked, nervously twining her hair through her fingers. "You're not going back to Fred's are you?''

"No, that would be too risky. But I do plan on staying hidden until the Zopo brothers are caught and are behind bars.''

A sudden noise made Courtney start nervously, but it was only Ryan dropping his bar of soap in the shower. She knew from personal experience that he loved long hot showers, the longer the better. But just to be on the safe side…

"Hold on just a sec, I'm going to switch to the phone in the living room." Throwing on her cotton robe, she raced to the living room. "Are you still there?''

"Yes. And I am still wondering how you are?''

"I'm fine," she assured him. "Ryan is taking good care of me."

"This is what I am afraid of." Anton's voice reflected his parental-like concern. "The two of you locked up in your small apartment."

"I'm not in my apartment now."

"How can that be?" He sounded confused. "I called you there."

She briefly filled him in on the break-in at her building, and at the attempted robbery at the bank. "Ryan tells me they should have the Zopos in custody any time now."

Anton snorted his skepticism. "I will believe that when I see it. Where are you?"

"I'm near Newport, on the coast."

He was clearly surprised and delighted with this news. "Me, too. You know how I love the ocean. But why are you here?"

"Ryan brought me to a beach house of a friend of his so I'd be safe."

"Safe, hah!" Anton scoffed. "I'll bet the scoundrel brought you to a love nest on the ocean. Tell me where you are and I will come there myself."

His words panicked her, stopping her in her tracks from the nervous pacing she'd been doing across the living room floor. "No, you can't!"

But he overrode her objections. "Yes, I can," he said righteously. "I will come to protect you before your love for him returns."

"It's too late," she admitted unsteadily. "I do love him. Maybe I never stopped loving him. I don't know what the future holds for us, but I know that he's the only man for me.''

''Oh, *malenka*.'' Anton's voice was sympathetic, as if he already knew she was doomed for heartbreak.

''I shouldn't keep you any longer,'' she said, belatedly realizing that the phone could still be tapped.

''Do not fear,'' Anton reassured her. ''All will be well. Try to get free of Ryan long enough to call me from a pay phone so we can talk longer. These short speeches are not enough. I am at the Sea Breeze Motel. Call me.''

''I'll try. I promise.''

As she retraced her steps back to the bedroom, she hoped this mess would be over soon. And if it was, if the Zopos were in custody and her uncle did decide to testify, would Ryan walk out of her life again? Had she kept her uncle on the phone too long? As she entered the bedroom, her worry about the authorities being able to trace her uncle's call became a moot issue.

Because Ryan was there, a towel hastily wrapped around his otherwise naked torso. The water may still have been running in the bathroom, but he was no longer in the shower. Instead he was standing next to the bedside table, with the phone receiver against his ear. From the look on his face it was obvious that he'd been eavesdropping on her conversation with her uncle, listening to every word on the bedroom extension.

Which meant he knew where her uncle was staying. He also knew that Courtney had just confessed she loved him. She could imagine which news Ryan considered to be the most important.

His voice could crack stone. "I notice you didn't try to convince your uncle to turn himself in."

Maybe that was all he noticed. No, Ryan never missed a thing. He'd heard, he'd registered. He just chose to ignore the information about her loving him because it was irrelevant to his case. Picking up a feather pillow from the bed, she whacked him over the head with it.

"What are you angry about? I'm the one who should be furious," he growled at her, trying to wrestle the pillow away from her.

She held on tight. In the end something had to give, and it was the pillow, ripping right down the middle, the way her heart felt like it was doing. Feathers flew everywhere as Courtney flew backward onto the bed.

Shoving her long hair out of her face, she blew a downy feather out of her mouth as she looked up at Ryan. How could she have been so weak? She'd known all along what he was up to, but like a stupid fool she'd let herself be swept away by rosy fantasies.

Like a vengeful mythical god, Ryan stood beside the bed, his hands on his lean hips as he glared down at her, fire in his hazel eyes. The towel wrapped around his waist had slipped dangerously low. His voice was as intimidating as his expression. "I don't have time to get into this with you now."

She tried to keep her voice from trembling. "What are you going to do?"

"My job." Turning his back on her, he picked up the phone, angrily punching out a number.

She numbly listened to him arrange with local law enforcement to have someone come to the beach house to keep an eye on her. So he was going to take her uncle in. She'd known he would. It had been foolish to think he'd do otherwise. It was his job, as he'd told her frequently. And he was good at what he did. He wasn't about to let anything get in the way of his goal. Including her.

As she looked at her surroundings through tear-streaked eyes she was hit by the undeniable fact that a leopard never changes its spots.

Pain spilled through her. She distantly heard him hang up the phone as she hurriedly wiped away her tears.

"Officer Logan will be here in five minutes," he told her curtly. "Until then, you'll stay right where you are, where I can make sure you don't try to double-cross me by calling your uncle and warning him."

"Double-crossing is more up your alley than mine," she accused, the betrayal cutting deep. Her words were choppy, her sentences abrupt. "You planned this entire thing."

"What are you talking about?"

"This." Sitting up, she angrily smacked the mattress with the open palm of her trembling hand. "You got me into bed and made love to me so that I'd let my guard down and lead you to my uncle."

All Ryan said was, "I had no way of knowing you'd talk to your uncle behind my back, although I should have guessed as much since this isn't the first time you've conspired with him."

She noticed he didn't deny her accusation of him

having sex with her to use her to get to Anton. He didn't bother defending himself from the truth. She read it in his face, in the tightening of his jaw.

In silence they got dressed and waited for Ryan's replacement to arrive. "Don't let her near the phone," he instructed Officer Logan. To Courtney he said, "I've got work to do." Then he was gone.

"I GIVE UP!" Muriel tossed her hands in the air, nearly flinging her magic wand through the mirrored bedroom ceiling.

"Fairy godmother's aren't allowed to give up," Hattie primly informed her. Today her hat was a perky straw affair with fresh flowers on the crown.

Aggravated, Muriel turned on her. "Says who, Miss Smarty-pants? Where is it written that we can't give up?"

"In the rule book." With a whisk of her wand, Hattie produced a thick volume that was almost as big as she was, and as fancy, with gilded pages and colorful calligraphic printing. Moving the pages with a wave of her wand, she riffled through until she found what she was looking for. "Right here, on page 3,333."

"We've already broken plenty of rules in that book. Plus we messed up the Zopo brothers' fancy equipment, so we've already interfered more than once."

Hattie glared at Muriel, not pleased by the reminder. "But we're not supposed to. We're supposed to act like proper fairy godmothers."

"Proper, hah!" Muriel gave a sharp laugh. "If we were proper we wouldn't be in this mess. We wouldn't have screwed up at the Knight triplets' christening and given each of the babies too much fairy dust.''

Betty looked like she wanted to bop both her sisters over their heads as she joined in the conversation for the first time. ''Can it, you two fussbudgets! We've got to put our heads together to correct the situation.''

''We're not supposed to interfere,'' Hattie repeated.

''We're not supposed to fail, either,'' Betty said sternly. ''And given a choice, I'd rather do the former than the latter.''

10

"I TOLD YOU I would take care of things," Caesar assured his brother as they sat in the back of a Creamy Delight ice-cream truck. *La Traviata* was playing quietly in the background from a boom box. Caesar sat in a perfect lotus yoga position on a plush maroon-and-navy-blue oriental rug on the floor. Despite their unusual surroundings, he looked as unruffled as ever, his black hair and thin mustache perfectly groomed.

"Buying this truck was a brilliant idea," Brutus agreed, glad to be out of the uncomfortable driver's seat with the loose spring that dug into his tailbone. The wooden stool was a little better. He'd never dream of joining his brother on one of his cherished prayer rugs. They were now parked in a quiet residential area. Brutus had been driving for what felt like hours. He was hot and he wanted a shower, but he didn't dare say anything. Caesar hated it when he whined.

"Using sophisticated equipment to track down Leva's niece was also a good idea of mine." Caesar frowned down at the locator box he held in his hands, his manicured fingernails gleaming. "I cannot believe it malfunctioned once we got to Newport." He gave the box a smack. "I put that tracking device on Knight's car myself. I know it was done *correctly*."

Brutus knew the words were meant as a cut to him, the brother who did nothing correctly. That seemed to be his lot in life. Now he was on the run from the law. Stella, his dainty flower, would know that he wasn't really the investment manager he'd claimed to be. He couldn't believe the way his life was going down the toilet.

A banging noise on the side of the truck made him jump. Caesar barely flinched.

"Hey, Mr. Ice-Cream Man," a young voice shouted. "Come out from in there!"

In an attempt to keep up appearances, Brutus was wearing a white coat like the previous owner had worn. Caesar, however, refused to do more than wear a white shirt, complete with designer tie and gold cuff links. Even sitting on the rug, he still managed to emanate power. "You go," Caesar ordered with a wave of his hand.

Brutus went to the glass sliding window built into the side of the truck and saw the pint-size rug rat who had nearly given him a heart attack. "Beat it, kid," he growled in his best villain voice. "We're closed."

Far from being intimidated, the kid put his hands on his hips and started bawling at the top of his lungs, his face turning brilliant red with his efforts.

Brutus panicked. He had to do something to shut the brat up. And fast! It would be ruinous for them to be the center of attention.

"Here." Brutus reached into the metal freezer compartment on his right and grabbed a box full of paper-wrapped ice-cream cones. "Take them. They're free. Just go away."

The tears immediately came to a stop as the boy moved closer to grab the box, only to stare down at it and frown. "I don't like this flavor."

"Fine. Give them back and I'll give you another box."

"My sister likes these." Tucking the box under his sturdy arm, he pointed to a photo on the menu posted on the outside of the truck. "Give me a box of the Double-Devil Cherry Toppers."

"You little extortionist!" Brutus's voice reflected both anger and admiration as he gave the boy what he wanted. "Come back in a few years, kid, my brother might have a job for you."

"You!" Anton, dressed in Bermuda shorts and a blue shirt, answered Ryan's knock. Ryan had deliberately stood to one side so that he wouldn't be visible through the motel door's peephole. Anton's angular features were flushed with agitation, his blue eyes reflected his surprise and ire as he immediately tried to shove the motel room door in Ryan's face.

But Ryan was one step faster, putting his foot in the threshold before shoving the door open. "Yeah, me. You were expecting maybe the Prize Patrol?"

"I was expecting you to show some intelligence," Anton berated him. "To show some honor."

"Yeah, right." Ryan entered the room and shut the door behind him. The motel room was small, the bathroom through the open archway even smaller. He was relieved to see that the only window was next to the entrance where he stood. "Like it was honorable of you to climb out that bathroom window."

"So that stuck in your craw, did it?" Anton smirked. "Good. You are entirely too cocky."

Ryan's eyes narrowed. "How would you know?"

"I know. And your behavior today just confirms my worst suspicions about you."

"That I'm good at my job?"

"That you put your job before all else," Anton stated.

Ryan scowled, thinking how much Anton sounded like Courtney. "Meaning what?"

"Meaning you left my niece alone in your decadent love nest, unprotected while the Zopo brothers are still on the loose."

"Let's get a few things straight." Ryan paused, not sure which thing to get straight first. There were so many. He started with the least relevant one first, ticking it off on his finger. "First off, I don't own a love nest—"

Anton immediately interrupted him. "Where is my niece?"

"In a safe place."

"Hah!" Anton scoffed.

"Don't you 'Hah!' me, mister," Ryan growled. "Do you know what you've put me through since you took off?"

"I know what you've put my niece through." Anton glared at him, his eyes eloquently conveying the message that he'd like to do Ryan bodily harm. "You're breaking her heart all over again."

Ryan felt guilt shoot through him. He knew he'd

hurt Courtney, but damn it—she'd hurt him. He'd thought he could trust her and she'd betrayed him by talking to her uncle behind his back. She knew how important it was that Ryan bring Anton back into protective custody. But she'd given her loyalty to Anton instead of to Ryan. She might say she loved him, but she sure didn't act like it.

Knowing how devious Anton was, Ryan was only too well aware that the older man had brought up Courtney's name in an effort to distract him. But it wouldn't work. Not this time. "I know what you're doing."

"And I know what you've done," Anton shot back with a meaningful glare.

Ryan refused to be fazed by Anton's words. "You're trying to distract me so you can make a quick getaway again. Well, it's not going to happen." Ryan took out the standard-issue handcuffs he'd had in the car and held them up threateningly. "Now you can come along willingly or we can make this difficult. It's up to you. Either way, consider yourself back in protective custody."

Anton waved his words away angrily. "That is not my main concern."

"Well, forgive me if it is mine," Ryan drawled.

"I will not forgive you," Anton shouted. "You are lower than a flea. My main concern is with my niece. And so would yours be if you were any kind of man. Who is protecting her while you are standing here?"

"You don't have to worry about Courtney," Ryan assured him. "I left her in the care of a local law enforcement officer."

The older man's eyes widened with incredulity. "How could you leave her safety to someone else?"

"Courtney is just fine. As stubborn as always, but safe."

"She better be—" Anton spoke the words with soft but unmistakable menace "—or your name will be mud."

COURTNEY HAD THE FEW things she'd brought with her packed and ready to go in the black backpack she used as a suitcase. Now that Ryan had captured her uncle, or was in the process of doing so, it would be back to business as usual as far as he was concerned. His time with her was up.

Even though Ryan had overheard her confess to her uncle that she loved Ryan, he still hadn't said a word. At least not about that. He'd had plenty to say about her messing up his case, but not about how he felt about her. He certainly hadn't said he loved her.

What was she expecting? A miracle? Would she never learn? With her long hair restrained in a tight bun, she curled up on the couch, watching the cold rain that had started to fall streak a path against the living room windows.

"So much for the sunshine," Officer Logan noted in an attempt to make conversation.

Courtney didn't have it in her to make small talk. Not now. The policeman seemed to recognize that fact, but that didn't stop him from doing his best to cheer her up. "How about a soda? Ryan said there were some in the fridge."

Ryan had said plenty, none of it what she wanted

to hear. The policeman was young. With his sandy hair and large ears, he reminded her of a rambunctious puppy eager to please. Even the expression in his brown eyes was earnest.

She didn't have the heart to disappoint him. "Sure," she said dully, "a soda would be fine."

"Great. I'll be right back."

She could have gotten the soda herself, or gone with him, but she seemed glued to her spot on the couch. She'd been curled up here, brooding about Ryan, since he'd left. Since then droplets of rain had run down the window like tears from heaven.

What an emotional roller-coaster ride she'd been on since Ryan had shown up in front of her desk at the Fell Federal Bank. There had been that initial shock and hope that he'd come to his senses and had come to declare his love for her. Then he'd told her about the case he was on, and she'd known. The only thing Ryan changed in his life were his socks and underwear, not his priorities.

Oh, sure he'd moved from Chicago to Oregon, but only because of his job. Not because of her. He probably hadn't even known she was in the same state. Probably hadn't cared. He'd told her that he hadn't wanted to work this case, that he was no happier about it than she was.

She didn't doubt that. But still he'd used the attraction that was between them to get what he wanted. And he wanted more than her in his bed. He wanted her uncle back in custody, wanted this blip on his no doubt spotless professional record cleared up.

She couldn't believe how she'd fallen into this

emotional trap. She'd tried to be so careful, so aware of what he was up to every step of the way. Then she'd fallen off the caution wagon big time, and taken a leap of faith that things between them would be different this time.

Speaking of time, she wasn't sure how much had passed since Officer Logan had gone to get that soda, but surely it was long enough by now. The house was large, but not that large. And the kitchen was just down the hall.

"You okay in there?" she called out.

"Just dandy." A strange man in a Creamy Delight ice-cream jacket walked into the living room. Beside him was a taller, more distinguished-looking man with a thin mustache. He was wearing a white shirt and black slacks. But the main thing that got her attention was the shiny gun in his hand.

"Who are you?" She tried to keep her voice steady and not make any sudden moves. Fear shot through her with stunning haste. "Where's Officer Logan?" Surely they hadn't harmed that poor young man?

"He is indisposed at the moment," the man with the gun said. "Tied up, you might say. In the pantry. As for who we are, would you care to make the introductions, Brutus or shall I?"

"You'd best do it, Caesar," the younger, heavier man nervously replied, tugging on his white ice-cream man jacket.

Caesar nodded his acquiescence. "But first I'd request that you slowly get off the couch and instead come sit in this straight-backed chair, Ms. Delaney." He waved his gun toward the piece of furniture.

Courtney's knees knocked as she got up from the couch and her legs were rubbery as she walked the short distance to the chair. Seconds later she was being tied up by Brutus. Introductions weren't necessary. These had to be the Zopo brothers.

While Brutus diligently wrapped a length of rope around her from shoulders to waist, his older brother bragged about their brilliance in tracking her down. "You were not easy to locate. Your uncle had told us nothing about you. An omission on his part, I'm sure." His white teeth gleamed beneath his thin dark mustache, making her think of a shark smiling right before taking a chomp out of someone. "And then those two missteps while my brother was in charge of this job. Hiring that idiot to grab you at the bank was one his poorer ideas, I'm afraid." He shot his brother a indulgent look laced with disdain. "As was that unfortunate break-in into the wrong apartment back in Fell. But then I took charge and turned things around."

Wanting to keep him talking, Courtney said, "And how did you do that?"

"By putting a tracking device on your boyfriend's car. Unfortunately there was a glitch once we reached Newport, and we were delayed a day cruising the area looking for his car. We found it early this morning. And waited for him to leave. Then it was simple to disarm the beach house security system. I am rather good at that sort of thing," he said, trying to look modest.

"How did you know I'd be with Ryan?"

"I saw the two of you leave your building together.

And I saw the way he looked at you. The man is crazy in love with you.''

Courtney couldn't believe what she was hearing. "You're wrong," she said flatly.

Caesar frowned at her. "You don't tell the people who are holding you captive that they are wrong. First rule in hostage situations. Now call Ryan on that beeper of his.''

"That might be rather difficult for me to do with my hands tied," she snapped.

"Difficult but not impossible. Tell me the number and I'll dial it," Caesar said.

Given her current situation—tied up with a gun aimed at her—she had no choice but to comply.

RYAN WAS JUST ABOUT to call headquarters with the news that he had Anton in his custody when his beeper went off. Glancing down at the display, he saw it was the beach house.

Must be Courtney paging him, wanting to know about her beloved, sneaky uncle. He could imagine what her frame of mind was. She was probably fit to be tied.

Keeping a wary eye on Anton, who was seated on the bed, Ryan stood nearby while punching out the numbers on the motel phone. When a man answered the phone, he almost hung up, thinking he'd dialed the wrong number.

"Ryan?" The silky voice made his voice run cold. "This is Caesar Zopo. I've got your girlfriend here. If you want to see her in one piece you'll bring Anton Leva over here. We'll trade her for him. You've got ten minutes.''

11

"TEN MINUTES?" Ryan repeated. It had taken him much longer than that to get to the motel from the beach house. "Wait—" But the dial tone was already buzzing in his ear.

Swearing, Ryan slammed down the phone and yanked Anton to his feet. There was no time to call in backup. He had to take care of this himself. Local law enforcement had already sent their most experienced officer to protect Courtney. But Officer Logan hadn't been able to complete his assignment.

Ryan prayed that he wouldn't be too late.

"What is wrong?" Anton's Czech accent was more noticeable as his agitation grew. Clearly he could tell that something was up. "Who was on the phone?"

"Your pals, the Zopo brothers."

"They are no pals of mine," Anton denied.

"Then you'd think you'd want to make sure they were put away for good."

Even as he spoke, Ryan was hustling Anton toward the car parked right outside. Stuffing him inside, Ryan had the car going before the door was even closed.

"Where are we going? Is it Courtney?" Anton's voice was filled with fear, a fear that was echoed in Ryan's heart.

"They've got her," Ryan said baldly.

He didn't even wince as Anton punched his arm. "I told you you shouldn't have left her!"

"Can it. We don't have time for this." Tires squealing, Ryan peeled the car out of the parking lot as he sped back to the beach house. "Courtney's life depends on doing this right."

Ryan had dealt with danger more times than he could count. But this time it was personal. Emotions shot through him, but he couldn't give in to them now. An image of Courtney sitting in this very car snapped into his mind. *Most people see trouble, they head in the opposite direction. But you, you run right into it.* He prayed like he'd never prayed before.

Anton gave him a long look before murmuring, "So you do love her after all. You have had a change of heart."

Was it really a change, Ryan wondered, or just a final admission of the truth he'd been fighting for so long? That the most important thing in his life was Courtney, not his job. That without her, life wouldn't be the joy it was with her. Everything would go back to dull gray and monotony. She was the color in his life, the cornerstone in his life, his reason for being.

Now he knew why he'd kept after her, provoking the old Courtney to come forward. Not because of the case. Not because he wanted her in his bed again. No, he'd wanted her back because, quite simply, she *completed* him. He needed her because he loved her and he loved her because she was Courtney—passionate, loyal, unique.

Ryan cursed that it took something like this—her being held hostage by the crazy Zopos—to make him come to his senses. But now that he had, he vowed he'd do whatever it took to keep her safe. Because she was his life.

"YOU HAVE THE PLANE all ready to leave?" Caesar was saying into his cellular phone. Courtney wasn't sure who he was speaking to, some minion in his employ maybe. She didn't even know where the airport was, but from his comments she judged it wasn't far away. "That is good. We should be there within the next half hour," he added, confirming her earlier suspicions. The Zopos planned on making their escape via the air. She wasn't sure how they planned on getting to the airport or what they planned on doing with her.

She doubted that Ryan would bring Anton here, despite their threats. It would go against everything he stood for, everything he'd been taught as a marshal. Not that Ryan would just abandon her to their clutches. He'd follow the rule book, do whatever was supposed to be done in hostage situations like this.

Flipping the cell phone closed, Caesar disconnected his call before strolling over to examine the leggy life-size andirons in the fireplace. "Interesting." He stroked his thin mustache with one perfectly manicured finger. "I wonder if there is a connection between the mermaid caught in the tangled fishnet up above the fireplace and these female legs down below. The imagery could be meant to convey that women are caught in the net of their own sex appeal, that the mermaid's siren call makes a victim of her as much as the hapless sailor she lures to his death."

Courtney shivered at his use of the word *death*. He was discussing this as if they were all at a trendy art gallery gathering, making pleasant conversation over champagne. She couldn't believe it.

"The sculpture outside was also most creative," Caesar continued. "But my tastes are not so... titillating. I prefer the classics. Are you a fan of opera, Ms. Delaney?"

She shook her head.

"Ah, that is too bad. You see, life is like opera. It is filled with moments of drama and greatness."

"With occasional intermissions to visit the bathroom," Brutus interjected.

Caesar shook his head regretfully. "My poor brother does not share my understanding or intellect."

"I was the one who thought up the idea of us leaving the country on a small plane," Brutus defended himself.

"Only because you get seasick on a boat. You still wanted to keep Anton Leva alive." Again, Caesar shook his head at him.

Brutus paled, his entire posture bowed in the face of his brother's displeasure. "I don't like violence," he muttered.

Courtney couldn't help wondering why he'd broken into her apartment building then, but didn't feel up to voicing her thoughts. She was too busy trying to loosen the knots on her ropes without being too obvious about it. She couldn't just sit here like a damsel in distress. But her options were rather limited at the moment.

"Once we are over the sea, we will just dump Leva out of the plane," Caesar said.

She froze, momentarily unable to believe what she was hearing. These men were calmly talking about killing her uncle! She was willing to bet they had a similar fate in store for her.

"It will be clean and simple," Caesar continued. "I am no fan of messy violence myself. I like to keep things neat." He brushed away a piece of lint from his pants before checking the face of his expensive watch. "Ryan and Anton should be here shortly. Brutus—" Caesar snapped his fingers and pointed at Courtney "—blindfold her."

She didn't like the sound of that at all. "No, wait!"

The command in her voice caught both Zopo brothers by surprise. Enough so that they paused. Well…Brutus paused, Caesar just stared at her.

"Don't blindfold me," she pleaded.

"Why not?" Caesar inquired with a tilt of his head.

"Because…I'm afraid of the dark." As an excuse, she was afraid it ranked right up there with telling Fred that Ryan was her half brother. That seemed like a lifetime away now. And if she didn't do something, she was afraid her lifetime would be over in the next few minutes.

"I am sorry to hear that," Caesar commiserated, giving her hope for a moment…only to add, "Blindfold her anyway, Brutus."

Brutus looked torn. "But she's afraid of the dark."

"I am not deaf," Caesar roared at Brutus. "Do as I tell you."

"It's not fair," Brutus muttered under his breath. "Mother always liked him best," he whispered to Courtney as if that explained everything.

Then her world went dark as a black silk scarf was tied around her eyes.

"Mother liked me best for a reason," Caesar said

arrogantly. "Because I am the brightest and the best."

A second later all hell broke loose.

Courtney shrank back against the chair as the room was filled with the sounds of crashes and curses. The hardwood floor in the living room magnified each noise to crescendo levels. Her heart was pounding in her ears, her breath coming in nervous gasps. If only she could *see*. But she could hear.

"That fishnet flew off the wall by itself," Brutus was shouting, his voice trembling. "Help me out, Caesar. The net is all over me. I can't get free!"

Another crash made Courtney flinch, her bare toes curling as if to make herself smaller, if not downright invisible.

"This place is haunted!" Brutus yelled.

"There is no such thing as ghosts," Caesar yelled back, but his voice was shaky. "Just keep ducking."

A thump, like a body falling on the floor, made her shriek nervously. This was followed by a thud that sounded painful. It was almost as if the Zopo brothers were engaged in a fight, but there was no indication of an assailant. She didn't hear anyone else's voice, nor did the Zopos say anything about another person being in the room. What on earth could be going on? Had Ryan's buddy booby-trapped the place?

"OH, HORSEFEATHERS! I missed him!" Hattie exclaimed after using her wand from her perch atop the stationary white ceiling fan to throw a seashell-filled glass lamp at Caesar.

"I told you that you needed to wear your glasses

for important moments like this," Muriel scolded from midair.

"Make sure he drops the gun," Betty instructed as she waved her wand over the fishing net that had captured Brutus, ensuring that he remained where he was, knocked unconscious by his own struggles to get loose. A big goose egg was already forming on his forehead where he'd hit it on the coffee table.

"You've got it." Taking aim, Muriel let loose, hitting Caesar dead center in the back of the head with a thick hardcover book on erotic art.

"Nice shot," Betty approved.

"Don't say that word. They could have shot Courtney." Hattie shuddered, fanning herself with her purple hat brimmed with lilacs and violets. "I can't believe we're doing this." Having said that, she tipped over the side of the fan blade, listing badly.

Tightening her baggy tan raincoat, Betty flew to her sister's side and propped her up. "Oh, for petunia's sake, this is no time for a fit of the vapors," she told Hattie in exasperation. "Muriel, help me out here," Betty shouted, as she and Hattie sank closer to the floor.

Muriel came to their aid, using her wand to move them to the safety of the mantelpiece. From there she admired their handiwork—Brutus unconscious, Caesar babbling incoherently. "Yes, I'd say things were progressing quite nicely."

RYAN PLANNED on using his cellular phone to alert the Zopos to the fact that he was in front of the beach house. He didn't want to do anything that would make them jumpy. Courtney's safety was his primary concern.

But he'd no sooner put the car in Park than he heard crashes coming from inside the house. Leaping out of the car, he was halfway up the walkway when the front door was thrown open and Caesar came racing out.

"Demons!" he babbled in terror, his thin mustache twitching, his eyes frantic. "After me. Trying to kill me!"

Ryan didn't take the time to ask questions. His arm shot out, felling Caesar with a powerful right hook. A second later, Ryan had him handcuffed to the metal fence post at the corner of the drive.

Hardly breaking stride, Ryan rushed into the house, his weapon drawn. Spotting Brutus unconscious on the floor, Ryan scanned the area for other assailants. Seeing Courtney tied up in a chair, he rushed to her side. "Are you okay?" he whispered as he undid her blindfold.

She nodded, thinking she'd never seen anything as beautiful as his face. She wanted to see his beloved lived-in face for the rest of her life—his thick brows, the curve of his long lashes, the stubborn line of his jaw and his sexy mouth. "How about you?" she whispered back.

"I'm fine." He cupped her face, as if needing to reassure himself that she was really unharmed. He also needed to make sure the threat was over. "How many of them are they?"

"Just two," she replied, still shaky, wincing as he undid the final knot on her ropes. "Brutus and Caesar.

But it sounded like an army came through here. Did you bring reinforcements? Is that what happened?''

''I have no idea what happened,'' he said, tenderly helping her to her feet. ''I'm just thankful it did.''

''I found the officer in the kitchen,'' Anton shouted from down the hallway. ''He is groggy but seems to be okay. I've called 911.''

''I was so scared.'' Courtney's voice was thick with tears. What a sap she'd be to cry now, when she was safe.

''Me, too,'' Ryan replied, his voice equally emotional as he reached out to lift a strand of her hair, which had come undone from the knot she'd done it in earlier, and slide it through his unsteady fingers. ''About what happened before…when we fought…what you said…ah, hell. You know I'm not good with this kind of thing, but you don't know…I haven't said…how much I love you.'' Now that he'd actually gotten the words out, they flowed in quick succession. ''When they called and told me they had you, there are no words to describe how I felt. You've always made me feel things I've never felt before. And maybe I've resented you for that. Maybe that's why I pushed you away in Chicago. But, honey, I'm not pushing you away ever again and that's a promise.''

To make his point, he gently took her in his arms, wrapping them around her with an intensity that said it all. Burying his face in her neck, he whispered his love for her over and over again. She felt the shudder run through his body and blinked the tears away.

Framing his face with her hands, she made him look at her. ''You already know that I love you. I've always loved you. There hasn't been anyone else for me.''

"You mean...?"

"I mean that you're my first and only lover. You may be incredibly stubborn and you may be married to your job—"

"I want to be married to you," he interrupted her to say. "You're the most important thing in my life. Not my job. I know that now."

His words caught her by surprise. She was still savoring the fact that he loved her. She could read the truth of that in his hazel eyes, feel it in his gentle embrace. But marriage...he'd always resisted that. She eyed him uncertainly. "Y-you're just...upset...because of what happened."

Shaking his head, he put a caressing finger to her lips, stilling her stumbling words. "I've never seen things more clearly in my life. I may be stubborn but I'm not stupid." His lopsided grin made her heart stop. "I've asked you to marry me. Now what do you say?"

"I say what took you so long?" Throwing her arms around his neck, she kissed him, secure in the knowledge that she was exactly where she belonged. She'd finally found her home, her security, and it was in the arms of the man she loved, the man who loved her. Her soul mate.

"I JUST LOVE happy endings," Hattie murmured tearfully from the living room mantelpiece. She'd restored her silvery curls and lilac hat to order with the help of her gilded mirror. Now her attention was focused on the embracing couple as she gazed at them with proud approval. "This makes me feel better than any amount of smelling salts could do."

"I admit it did turn out well," Betty agreed, reaching into the pocket of her baggy tan trench coat to haul out a big hankie. Blowing her nose in it, and surreptitiously wiping away a tear of her own, she said, "I did enjoy flexing a little fairy godmother muscle by besting those bad guys. Imagine someone not believing in ghosts."

"They probably don't believe in fairy godmothers, either," Muriel added, her smile as big as the Pacific Ocean. Ryan was her charge and her own personal favorite. Her heart was filled with satisfaction and happiness that he'd found his soul mate. "Believing is hard to come by these days. Most people don't."

"More fools them," Betty stated emphatically. "Congratulations on a job well done, Muriel. It was fun, but now it's time to move on to our next assignment."

Leaving it to Muriel to make what was becoming their signature statement. "Two down, one to go. Now let's go work on Anastasia."

Don't miss Anastasia's story,
TOO SMART FOR MARRIAGE,
in September 1998,
Love & Laughter #51

LOVE & LAUGHTER™

Marriage Makers

by
Cathie Linz

Once upon a time, three bumbling fairy god-mothers set out to find the Knight triplets their soul mates. But… Jason was too sexy, Ryan was too stubborn and Anastasia was just too smart to settle down.

But with the perfect match and a little fairy dust…
Happily Ever After is just a wish away!

March 1998—
TOO SEXY FOR MARRIAGE (#39)

June 1998—
TOO STUBBORN TO MARRY (#45)

September 1998—
TOO SMART FOR MARRIAGE (#51)

Available wherever Harlequin books are sold.

Take 4 bestselling love stories FREE

a FREE surprise gift!

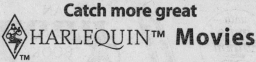
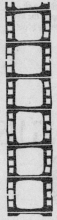

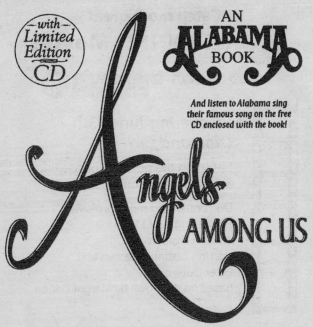

HARLEQUIN ULTIMATE GUIDES™

A series of how-to books for today's woman.

Act now to order some of these extremely
helpful guides just for you!

*Whatever the situation, Harlequin Ultimate Guides™
has all the answers!*

Presents
Extravaganza

25 YEARS!

It's our birthday
and we're celebrating....

Twenty-five years of romance fiction
featuring men of the world and captivating women—
Seduction and passion guaranteed!

Not only are we promising you three months of terrific
books, authors and romance, but as an added **bonus**
with the retail purchase of two Presents® titles,
you can receive a special one-of-a-kind keepsake.
It's our gift to you!

Look in the back pages of any Harlequin Presents® title,
from May to July 1998, for more details.

Available wherever Harlequin books are sold.

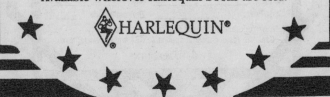 HARLEQUIN®